So Soon Done For

Also by Marian Babson:

Murder on a Mystery Tour
Death in Fashion
Death Swap
Trail of Ashers
Cruise of a Deathtime
Fool for Murder
Death Beside the Sea
Death Warmed Up
Bejeweled Death
Line Up for Murder
Dangerous to Know
Twelve Deaths of Christmas
The Lord Mayor of Death
Murder, Murder, Little Star

MARIAN BABSON

So Soon Done For

Walker and Company
New York

Copyright © William Collins Sons & Co Ltd 1979

All rights reserved. No part of this book may be reproduced or transmitted in any form or by any means, electronic or mechanical, including photocopying, recording, or by any information storage and retrieval system, without permission in writing from the Publisher.

All the characters and events portrayed in this story are fictitious.

Published in the United States of America in 1988 by the Walker Publishing Company, Inc.

Library of Congress Cataloging-in-Publication Data

Babson, Marian.
   So soon done for.

   Reprint. Originally published: London : Collins, 1979.
I. Title.
PS3552.A25S6   1988   813'.54   88-23
ISBN 0-8027-5694-8

Printed in the United States of America

10 9 8 7 6 5 4 3 2 1

If I were to be
  So soon done for,
I don't know what
  I was begun for.

                Epitaph on children's
                tombstones in old
                cemeteries.

CHAPTER I

They came in the night, like thieves. The children discovered them first and, through the children, the parents.

Sylvia rang Kay, Kay rang Alice, Alice rang Marjorie; meanwhile, Sylvia had rung the police and come back to Kay again.

'Can you imagine?' she wailed. 'The police say there's nothing they can do. No crime has been committed.'

'I don't suppose it has.' Kay tried to be comforting. 'It only counts as trespass, doesn't it?'

'That's what the police said.' Sylvia's voice rose. It was apparent that she would not be comforted. 'It isn't even strictly illegal – think of it! And the police said they couldn't do anything about it on *my* complaint because *I* don't own the house in question.'

'It's up to the Norrises to get a Court Order, I believe,' Kay said. 'They'll be back eventually and take care of it.'

'Eventually!' Such a distant prospect was of no use to Sylvia. 'And what are we to do in the meantime?'

'We could try to keep calm – ' Kay began, but was immediately interrupted. The question had been rhetorical.

'Calm?' Sylvia shrieked. 'With squatters in Crozier Crescent? I never thought I'd see the day!'

'It may not be so bad – ' Kay tried again.

'Bad? When a pack of scruffy strangers can walk in and take over someone else's home? How much worse can things get?'

'It isn't as if the Norrises were there very much – ' Kay found herself pushed into the position of almost defending the unseen squatters. That was the trouble with

Sylvia – she over-reacted so violently that people had to search for the best of the other side of the question in an attempt to restore some sense of balance. 'They've been in the West Indies for three months and they were in Switzerland before that.'

'That isn't the point.' Sylvia refused to look at any other side of the question. 'That people could move into their home in their absence – '

'*One* of their homes,' Kay murmured.

'Their *home*,' Sylvia continued firmly. 'It can't be allowed. Something must be done about it.'

'What do you suggest?' Kay asked. Sylvia ignored the question.

'I blame Marjorie,' she said. Sylvia always blamed Marjorie. It was as though she felt that having a lecturer in sociology resident in the Crescent were tantamount to having a disturbed adolescent in an area of intense poltergeist activity. Somehow, Marjorie was to blame for every social phenomenon that had erupted since she moved in, rather as though she had deliberately conjured them out of the atmosphere. 'Things like this never happened when old Mrs Albee was living here.'

Kay spent a silent moment debating whether to point out that, at eighty-five, old Mrs Albee could hardly have been expected to hurl herself into the fray of social revolution, or whether she should treat the remark as the *non sequitur* it undoubtedly was.

'But it's the deceit I object to most of all,' Sylvia went on. 'Those children – those grubby, disgraceful brats – '

Kay spared a complacent glance into the living-room where Emma, a peaches-and-cream child who had never caused a moment's concern, was placidly watching television.

'Do you realize those children – ? Children! – dreadful little monsters!' Sylvia's shudder was apparent, even over the telephone. 'Do you realize the – the *corruption* they carry with them? Why, they've already spread their poison. They told Rupert not to tell me – *me*, his own mother – that they'd moved into the Norris house. He'd been playing with them – secretly – every day for more than a week before I discovered it. They told him that if I found out about them, I'd forbid him to play with them,' Sylvia snarled. 'They were dead right there!'

Unexpectedly, Kay felt a pang for the unknown squatter children, so wise in the ways of a world they had never made. They were not, like other children, unsure of their welcome; they knew only too well that there would be no welcome for them in any neighbourhood they moved into. The manner in which they had gained their slow accretion of bitter knowledge did not bear thinking about.

'Teaching *our* children *their* deceit,' Sylvia stormed on. 'You can see what – '

'How *did* you find out?' Kay asked curiously. 'I had no idea the Norris house was occupied and I've walked past there every day. Of course, they've got that sign posted on the front door now, but now that they've been discovered, they might as well. Until you phoned this morning, I'd had no idea – '

'Precisely!' Sylvia said triumphantly. 'They were obviously planning to get away with it for as long as they could. If it hadn't been for the fact . . .' Her voice dropped, trailed off.

'What fact?' Kay prompted, intrigued. It was not often that Sylvia was speechless. 'What happened?'

'Oh, well,' Sylvia appeared to have developed an unnatural reticence. 'It was just that . . .'

'Just what?'

'Well, it wasn't *just* – ' Sylvia's voice rose to a crescendo of indignation. 'While Rupert was having his breakfast this morning, I caught him . . . well, *scratching*.' Despite her righteous indignation, the admission seemed dragged from her. 'Naturally, I burnt the clothes he'd been wearing yesterday, and I shampooed his hair three times in a row –

'It isn't funny!' She caught Kay's muffled snort and interpreted it correctly. 'Who knows *what* those disgraceful creatures may have brought into Crozier Crescent with them? And this was always such a *nice* place. We've got to *do* something.'

'What do you suggest?' Kay asked for the second time.

'Come over for drinks tonight,' Sylvia said. 'I'm asking everyone.'

'A council of war?' Kay was dubious.

'Seven-thirty,' Sylvia said decisively, although Kay suspected that the invitation had popped out on the spur of the moment.

'I'll phone the others now.' Unwittingly, Sylvia confirmed the suspicion. 'If we all put our heads together, *someone* must come up with some solution. And the men will be home. After all, just because they aren't here all day – most of them – it isn't fair to let us carry the whole burden of – '

In the living-room, Emma, still intent on the television programme, raised one hand to her head and scratched with uninhibited vigour.

'I must ring off now, Sylvia,' Kay said. 'I'll see you this evening. And, you're right, I'll see that Crispian comes, too.'

Before Sylvia could say anything more, Kay replaced the receiver and advanced grimly upon her unsuspecting daughter.

CHAPTER II

Rupert opened the door, having obviously been dragooned into acting as the little-gentleman-doorman for the occasion. Above a dazzlingly white shirt, his face had an unnaturally pink scrubbed look.

'Good evening, Rupert,' Crispian said, guiding Kay and Emma past the door. 'How are you?'

'My head hurts,' Rupert said, slamming the door behind them.

'So does mine.' Emma raised her hand to the yellow thistledown floating from her scalp, encountered her mother's watchful eye, and lowered the hand again. She and Rupert exchanged glances.

'You're the last to arrive!' Sylvia hovered in the doorway beyond them, accusing even as she greeted them. 'You two run along upstairs.' She shifted her gaze to Emma and Rupert. 'Barnaby is waiting for you in the playroom, and everyone else is here now.'

Kay and Crispian followed her into the living-room. While they greeted the others, Jeremy was jittering at the bar. He signalled to Crispian urgently.

'Gin and tonic, thanks. For both of us.' Crispian crossed over to collect their drinks.

But Jeremy was uninterested in their preferences. 'God! What a day at the Agency!' He picked up one bottle after another, lifting each one a few inches off the tray and setting it back again, like a bell-ringer in an old Music Hall turn. 'We had a Presentation for the most important client – and he didn't let on by a flicker of an eyelash whether he liked it or not. Just "Thank you, gentlemen", and he walked out. I've had three tranquillizers since lunch – and then I come home to *this!*' He swung a bottle of Pernod out to indicate the roomful of people, then lifted it and squinted at the label.

'I say, old boy, do you think I dare risk it?' He glanced at Crispian for reassurance. 'I know one oughtn't to mix drink and drugs – but it's been *hours* since my last tranquillizer. And I can't face an evening like this on a glass of tomato juice.'

'You could try another tranquillizer,' Crispian suggested, but Jeremy wasn't listening. He replaced the Pernod, rang a carillon with Scotch and brandy, then took up the gin, swinging it in a dinner bell 'come-and-get-it' stroke.

'Don't call us, we'll call you,' Crispian murmured.

'What?' Still absorbed in his own problems, Jeremy looked at Crispian as though just realizing he was there. 'Sorry, old man, you wanted gin and tonic, didn't you?' Meticulously, he poured a drink, gulped at it, and handed Crispian the bottle. 'Help yourself,' he said and stared meditatively across the room.

Crispian poured drinks for himself and Kay. Jeremy, he noted, had given himself a treble. One for each tranquillizer, presumably. Adding tonic – a refinement Jeremy had neglected – Crispian carried the drinks over to join Kay.

She had taken the last space on the sofa, next to Alice and Arthur. Crispian handed Kay her drink and perched beside her on the arm of the sofa.

'What *I* want to know – ' Sylvia was in full cry – 'is how they came *here*. I mean, Crozier Crescent is such a secluded cul-de-sac. That's why we like it. It's so out of the way. No one would even know it existed unless they were actually looking for it.'

'I see what you mean.' Arthur nodded. 'It isn't as though they'd gone to ground in one of those empty flats in Cardinal Avenue. Anyone could have noticed they were unoccupied, Cardinal Avenue being right on the bus route – '

'Exactly!' Sylvia cut in triumphantly. 'Crozier Crescent is a place one would have to *know* about. It's not a place they could have stumbled over by accident – '

Unfortunately, Candice Carson chose that moment to giggle. She tried to stifle it instantly, looking to her husband, Nick, as though he might be able to persuade the others that it had really been a cough she intended.

'It's all very well,' Sylvia said severely, 'for *some* people to laugh. People with nothing at stake – '

Which was hitting below the belt, underlining the fact that the Carsons were newcomers to Crozier Crescent, newly-weds with no family, and perhaps not even people who would remain for very long, Nick's company being notorious for moving staff around the country – and sometimes the world – at short notice and with no concern for the long-term effects on those involved.

'People who have no intention of putting down *roots* – ' Sylvia's tone relegated them to a rank barely above that of squatters themselves.

'You're right,' Nick said, rushing in to try to retrieve his bride's blunder. 'About knowing where empty houses are, I mean. They have organizations, haven't they, who issue mimeographed lists of addresses of empty houses? Somehow, the Norris house must have got on to one of those lists.'

'But *how*? That's what I want to know.' Sylvia's gaze hovered delicately just above Marjorie's head. '*Who* could have told them about the Norris house?'

Marjorie continued sipping her sherry with a placid smile. Jeremy rattled the bottles at the bar again, lifting each one again and peering at it intently. Searching for the lost chord, perhaps.

'*And*,' Sylvia continued accusingly, 'how long will it be before more of their friends join them? Before none of us dares to go out, not even to the shops, for fear of coming back and finding our homes occupied by . . . *them*?'

'Oh, I don't think the situation is so bad as that,' Marjorie said calmly. 'That *would* be more than the law would let them get away with – and they'd know it. Besides, you have no basis for such a statement. We've seen no signs that these squatters are part of a larger group, nor that they're likely to be the spearhead of a mass invasion. Personally, I should doubt it. I believe that what we have here is merely an isolated incident.'

'Oh, "*merely*" – ' Sylvia glared at Marjorie with renewed suspicion. 'An "isolated *incident*". How *comforting*.'

Even some of the others began viewing Marjorie with suspicion at this point. She would not be incapable, they felt, of setting the cat among the pigeons – and then sitting back and making notes on behavioural patterns. *Had* she set the squatters in their midst? And was she, behind that bland exterior, silently laughing at their alarm?

'It's always nice,' Sylvia underlined in dulcet tones, 'to have an *expert* opinion on these matters.'

Kay began to wonder whether the pigeon had not been set down in the midst of the cats. Momentarily, she felt sorry for the squatters. They began to seem not so much menacing as menaced. Marjorie, too, seemed to be in danger of collecting a few claw marks.

'I have at least spoken to them,' Marjorie said quietly. 'I should rather imagine that's more than you've done.'

'What?' Sylvia had been about to sit down, now she straightened up and advanced on Marjorie. 'When?'

'This morning,' Marjorie said. 'I was posting a letter when I met Elf on her way back from the shops. Naturally, I spoke to her.'

'Naturally,' Sylvia said bitterly. 'You wouldn't let an opportunity like that pass, would you?'

Jeremy dropped a clanger, perhaps to distract attention from Sylvia's unchecked rudeness, or perhaps because the tranquillizers and gin had begun their uneasy battle.

A decapitated bottle of tonic water lay on its side at his feet, its contents pumping out across the carpet like blood from a severed artery.

'Oh, Jeremy!' Sylvia flew for a mopping-up cloth. Jeremy retrieved the bottle on his second try and set it upright on the bar.

'Elf – ' Alice said wonderingly. 'Can anyone really be named Elf?'

'It was the only name she gave,' Marjorie spoke dispassionately. 'Short for Elfrida, I imagine. Although I understand some of them call themselves Mickey Mouse – or Minnie – when they're questioned. Not that I questioned her. I simply passed the time of day.'

'You *do* seem to be well up on these things.' Candice had evidently decided it was time she showed more concern about the situation, and further decided that it was wiser to weigh in on Sylvia's side.

'But *why* did you even speak to the creature?' Sylvia demanded despairingly, coming back into the room. 'Surely the best thing is to ignore them all utterly?'

Jeremy snatched the cloth she was holding and dropped to his knees, as though hurling himself out of the range of fire. He mopped violently at the carpet, head down, dissociating himself from the proceedings.

'Do you really think so?' Marjorie had the disconcerting habit of turning the question back on the questioner. Furthermore, she always gave the impression of being deeply interested in the answer. Noting it down, in fact. Especially when talking with Sylvia. They might all be going to figure in some future tome on sociology in the suburbs, but surely Sylvia was going to have a chapter all to herself.

'Yes, I do.' Sylvia hesitated, the technique was infectious. 'What do *you* think we ought to do?'

Jeremy lurched to his feet and beamed at them all

with professional affability. The soggy cloth remained on the carpet and Sylvia might have spoken sharply about it had she not been occupied with other worries at the moment.

'Perhaps,' Alice suggested timidly, 'we could get up a petition asking them to go away?'

'Do you really think they'd go?' Now it was Alice who flinched away from the laser beam of Marjorie's undivided attention.

'Well, they ought to . . .' Alice looked around for support. 'If they understood that we didn't want them here . . .' She faded out. The eldest of them – Barnaby was her grandson – she had been brought up in a different world. Now she found herself one of the over-civilized, unable to cope with the problem of dealing with those who recognized no laws, responded to no social pressure.

'What do *you* think we ought to do?' Sylvia repeated.

'I think – ' Marjorie studied her glass carefully, then raised her eyes – 'I think we ought to befriend them.'

'*Befriend* them!' Sylvia's voice rose an octave. 'Are you *mad*? What do you mean by that?'

'I mean – ' Marjorie didn't bother to look around for support. The battle was between herself and Sylvia. 'I mean, make friends with them, invite them into our homes, draw them back into the social structure of the community.'

'You *are* mad,' Sylvia said flatly. She rounded on her husband. 'Jeremy, talk to her. *Do* something.'

Jeremy took another drink.

Kay and Crispian exchanged a worried glance. Jeremy was already fairly glassy-eyed and he had poured another treble.

'Jeremy – ' Sylvia had a warning note in her voice.

'Certainly. Assuredly.' Jeremy beamed another professional smile around the room, although it was uncertain whether he realized the audience consisted of his neighbours rather than his clients.

'Gentlemen. Oh, and ladies.' He sketched an unsteady bow. 'I think you will all agree that the Presentation you are about to see – '

'No! No!' Sylvia snapped.

'No?' Jeremy looked around vaguely. 'Oh yes, of course. That was this afternoon.' His smile was a masterpiece of rueful apology. 'Sorry. What I mean to say is, the question before the Board – '

He stopped automatically at the hiss of Sylvia's indrawn breath. 'Sorry,' he apologized again. He looked at Sylvia. 'What *is* the question?'

'Marjorie,' Sylvia said between clenched teeth, 'wants us to make friends with those filthy squatters. She thinks we ought to invite them into our homes.'

Jeremy stood perfectly still for a moment, as though contemplating all angles of the problem, then slowly pitched forward on to his face.

CHAPTER III

'Strange. That's the first time I've ever seen Jeremy as overtired as a newt,' Crispian said thoughtfully as they re-entered their own house. 'Usually, he can hold his drink. I wonder what kind of tranquillizers he's been taking.'

'The latest, knowing Jeremy.' Kay encouraged Emma towards the stairs with a little push. 'Probably something so new they're not on the market yet. Doesn't his agency have one of the big drug companies as an account?'

'Quite a good-sized one, but not one of the biggest,' Crispian corrected, still looking thoughtful. 'Whatever it is, I hope it's been tested properly. Jeremy was looking quite odd even before he took a drink. I can't think *that* new product is on the way to being one of their more successful items.'

'After all, Jeremy had had quite a tiring day, by the sound of it.' Kay frowned at Crispian. Emma was listening avidly behind a façade of inattention. In fact, the more inattentive Emma appeared, the more closely she was actually following what was going on.

'Of course,' Crispian said drily. Kay glanced anxiously at Emma – tone of voice could convey as much as words – but Emma appeared momentarily preoccupied by something outside the window.

'Please may I go out to play?' Emma asked cautiously.

'It's nearly time for bed,' Kay said quickly. She too had caught a glimpse of a tousled head outside. Tousled – or uncombed?

Perhaps there was something to be said for Marjorie's idea of befriending the squatters. Once an amicable relationship had been established, one could drop hints about cleanliness – possibly even shampoo the children oneself, thus taking care of one problem at source, as it were.

'How many children *are* there over there?' Kay asked abruptly.

Emma deliberately gave her a look of blank incomprehension.

Kay felt a surge of fury and dismay, so intermingled they could not be disentangled. Was this, then, what Sylvia really feared: the implications of deceit, the burgeoning of new loyalties to replace family loyalties, the beginning of growing up – and growing away?

'I don't know,' Crispian said innocently. 'Didn't Sylvia have them all tabbed?'

'Not you!' Kay snapped. 'I'm talking to Emma – and she knows it!'

'I don't know.' Belatedly, Emma answered the original question. Once again, her very blankness proclaimed the lie. She knew how many children there were in the Norris house, and she knew how many adult squatters had taken up residence there. Probably she had even been inside talking to them, perhaps even sharing their food with them. She and Rupert.

'Oh, don't you?' Kay was aware of the faint placatory noises Crispian was beginning to make, but she ignored them. 'Well, perhaps I can find out for myself.' She strode to the door and threw it open.

'Come in,' she called. 'Come in here. I know you're out there!'

'Oh, really,' Crispian protested. 'When Marjorie said befriend them, I don't think she meant tonight.'

'Come on.' Kay consciously softened her voice. 'Emma can't come out to play, it's too late. But, if you come in, you can have a glass of milk and some biscuits with her before she goes to bed.'

There was silence from the shrubbery, then a twig

moved, and another.

'Hurry up,' Kay said. 'You can only have ten minutes, then Emma goes to bed.'

The implied promise of a curfew to be thwarted worked its inevitable magic. A grubby blonde head appeared, followed by a dark curly one. Somewhere between them bobbed a mousy head on a small mousy – thoroughly indeterminate – child.

The eldest was unmistakably English, ivory and flaxen underneath the grime. She slid past Kay quickly, with a sideways glance – and a curious defensive twist of her body, like a stray dog cringing away from an expected kick.

The middle girl was café-au-lait. A child with problems she had not encompassed yet, and who seemed curiously unaware of them, meeting the world – and Kay's eyes – with a trusting smile.

The third child remained indeterminate, even on closer inspection. Probably English, probably light brown hair, probably friendly. Perhaps indifferent would be a better word for her than indeterminate.

Emma came up behind Kay and moved, as though crossing an invisible barrier, to stand ranged with her friends. They stood in a row looking at Kay as though waiting for instructions. (Or as though facing a common enemy.)

'Aren't you going to introduce me to your friends?' Kay asked the hostile Emma.

'This is Poppy . . .' Emma indicated the eldest girl reluctantly, as though suspecting some trick. 'And this is Jasmine . . .' The dusky child offered an enchanting grin. 'And this is Heather . . .' The youngest remained indifferent.

Kay felt Crispian move up behind her just before his hand rested encouragingly on her shoulder. They faced the children like soldiers drawn up in line of battle – adversaries.

'Biscuits?' Jasmine reminded her of the promise that had lured them into the house. '*Chocolate* biscuits?' she wheedled.

'Of course.' Kay returned the smile without great effort. 'This way.' She turned and led them into the kitchen.

'Just a minute – ' She halted them as they scrambled for chairs at the kitchen table. 'Emma – wouldn't you like to show your guests to the bathroom, so that they can wash their hands before they eat?'

Four suspicious faces turned towards her. Emma's with a furious glare. But Kay was more interested in the effect her words had had on Poppy, the eldest.

After the first startled glance, Poppy's gaze lowered and she furtively assessed her own grimy hands, then she looked up again to meet Kay's gaze blandly.

'I was just going to ask,' Poppy assured her, carefully hiding her dirtier hand behind her back. 'These kids – ' she waved the comparatively clean hand towards the others – 'get so dirty. Out playing all day – '

'Off you go, then,' Kay said. 'Emma will show you the way.' Perhaps they could *all* show them the way. Poppy seemed to be a quick learner. Perhaps, after all, Marjorie's idea was the right way to go about things.

She opened a packet of chocolate fingers and set milk and glasses on the table to the accompaniment of distant sounds of muted splashing. She hesitated, then heard a faint joyous giggle. More decisively, she ripped open a packet of bourbon creams and one of Viennese wafers and tipped them on to the plate It wasn't the children's fault and probably they had had few enough parties in their young lives.

The children returned: Emma apparently mollified by

the attitude of her friends towards soap and water, since they appeared to regard it as a frivolous luxury and not the dreary chore it seemed to herself and such contemporaries as Rupert. Indeed, Poppy was swaggering slightly, glowing with accomplishment, and Jasmine, damp tendrils framing her face, looked happier than ever at the turn of events. Not even the baby appeared to resent the intrusion of hygiene upon her unprepared experience.

'Sit down,' Kay greeted them.

'Yes, sit down.' Emma took over as hostess. 'Have some biscuits.' She passed the plate to her guests.

A cold look from Poppy abruptly inhibited the eagerness with which the others snatched for the biscuits. Under her quelling gaze, their outspread hands contracted and they settled for one genteel biscuit apiece.

'You can have all you want,' Kay comforted. 'There's no rush.' It was a direct contradiction of her earlier assertion that Emma had to go to bed soon, but none of the children appeared to notice.

'These are nice,' Poppy said, in an oddly adult social tone, speaking to Kay rather than to Emma.

'I'm glad you like them,' Kay said.

'Oh, I do. I think your bathroom is very nice, too.' Poppy hesitated, then added proudly, '*We* have a blue bathtub.'

'You mean the Norrises have a blue bathtub!' The words were out before Kay had time to think, an indignant reflex against the manner and circumstances of the intrusion of these strangers into their peaceful neighbourhood. As soon as she said them, Kay knew they were a mistake.

Poppy withdrew into herself, her face went blank, her eyes lost all expression. She set down her milk and pushed back her chair.

'Thank you for the biscuits and milk,' she said. 'We have to go now.'

'Oh no,' Kay's voice rose over the muttered protests of the other children. 'Have another biscuit.'

'No, thank you.' Poppy glowered a silent command at her sisters. 'We have to go now,' she repeated stubbornly.

Kay watched them helplessly, realizing that ordinary blandishments and bribes were useless against such determination. Poppy was not an ordinary child – how could she be with the life she must have led?

'Well, come again another time,' she called to their retreating backs.

'Another time,' Poppy echoed without turning around.

'Bad luck,' Crispian murmured. 'And you'd got off to such a flying start.'

'I couldn't help it,' Kay said. 'Something just snapped when she began talking like that. As though she *owned* the Norrises' house, as though they'd bought and paid for everything in it – '

'They don't know any better,' Crispian said. 'They're just children.'

'I know.' Kay turned to him despairingly. 'That's why I shouldn't have behaved like that. It isn't *their* fault.'

They heard the slam of the front door and Emma's running footsteps. 'You were awful!' Emma stormed into the kitchen. 'You were just awful to my friends! I hate you!' She turned and ran out. They heard her footsteps dashing up the stairs to her room.

'It's all gone wrong,' Kay said. 'Everything. I wanted to be nice to them and then ask them questions. Now I've just alienated them – and Emma, too – and we haven't learned a thing.'

'Never mind,' Crispian comforted. 'Those children were born alienated, and Emma gets over her moods quickly. You can try again another time.'

'Yes,' Kay smiled weakly. 'They'll still be around,

won't they? They're not going to vanish overnight.'

'Highly unlikely,' Crispian said. 'Not when they've fallen into something as cushy as the Norris pad. So let's get a good night's sleep and worry about it in the morning. Tomorrow is another day.'

CHAPTER IV

Kay glimpsed Sylvia several times from the kitchen window as she was preparing breakfast next morning. Each time, Sylvia was watering her window-boxes, cautiously inserting the long nozzle amongst the blooms as though she expected to encounter a meths drinker bedded down on the moss. Perhaps she did. ('Once a neighbourhood begins to deteriorate . . .')

Each time, also, Sylvia was surreptitiously surveying the Crescent, paying a great deal more attention to the comings and goings of her neighbours than to the watering. By the time Kay sat down with her family to breakfast she feared that the flowers in the window-boxes must be going down for the third time.

When she opened the front door to speed Emma on her way to school, Sylvia was hovering – with Rupert – outside on the pavement.

'You're *not* letting Emma go to school by herself!' Sylvia said accusingly.

'She's been going to school by herself for a long time,' Kay said. 'You know that.'

'I know,' Sylvia said. 'But *now*!'

'What's so different about – ?' Then Kay remembered. She had not actually forgotten, it was just that the knowledge came and went. It was not quite the world-shaking event to her that it obviously was to Sylvia.

'*I'm* taking Rupert to school myself,' Sylvia said virtuously. 'I thought I'd wait and take Emma as well. I was afraid you wouldn't think of it.'

'Hello, Rupert,' Emma said. She walked down the path and joined him with suspicious docility.

'That's very thoughtful of you, Sylvia,' Kay said drily.

She forbore to point out that it was by way of locking the stable door. The children had already made contact and there were many more opportunities and places for them to meet than on the way to school. In any case, it was doubtful that the squatter children ever went anywhere near a school. It was also unlikely that they went to bed early enough to be up and about at this hour of the morning.

'I thought we might take turns.' In a vague way, Sylvia seemed aware of some of the pitfalls herself. 'I don't mind taking them to school in the morning, and if you'd just collect them both in the afternoon – '

'For how long?' Kay tried to introduce a note of reality.

'Why – ' The blank look on Sylvia's face betrayed that she had not thought very far ahead. 'Why, until we get this situation cleared up, of course.'

'That could take weeks,' Kay said gently. 'Or months. Possibly even – '

'Rupert! Emma!' Sylvia cut across her sharply. 'You two start walking ahead – but *slowly*. I'll catch up with you in a minute.'

Carefully avoiding each other's eyes, Emma and Rupert moved off at a snail's pace. Sylvia waited grimly until, despite their best efforts, they were out of earshot, before turning back to Kay.

'I cabled the Norrises yesterday,' Sylvia said. 'I sent a Night Letter. We ought to be hearing something today. Perhaps,' she added wistfully, 'they'll fly back.'

'Perhaps,' Kay agreed without conviction. She looked beyond Sylvia, noting that Emma and Rupert, now some distance ahead, had begun talking earnestly together.

'Where are they?' Sylvia spun round. 'Wait a minute!' she called after them. 'Rupert, wait for Mummy!'

Imperceptibly, Emma and Rupert lengthened their strides.

'We *must* talk about this – ' Sylvia turned back to Kay. 'Make some plans – ' She twisted around to look after the children; once they rounded the corner, they would be out of sight. She danced nervously from foot to foot, unwilling to go without having settled her point, yet reluctant to linger and let the children escape her.

'Come over to our place tonight – ' Sylvia started in pursuit of the children. 'I should have heard from the Norrises by then. I'll contact the others and get as many together as I can.'

No one answered the bell, but the front door stood invitingly ajar. After a suitable interval, Kay pushed it open and entered. Rupert glared at her balefully from the top of the stairs and, seeing that Emma wasn't with her disappeared from view. Kay gave a mental shrug and moved on towards the living-room.

'Don't come in!' The anguished shriek halted her in the doorway. 'Don't move! Just stand there!'

And let me look at you. But that wasn't the end of the sentence. No one was looking at her – once she had halted. Quite the contrary.

Jeremy, Sylvia, Candice and Nick were sprawled across the carpet on all fours in varying attitudes of supplication.

'Lost one again, have you?' Kay asked unfeelingly.

'I sneezed – ' Jeremy patted the carpet in front of him frantically, inching forward cautiously as he did so. 'One tiny little sneeze – my hay fever, you know – and it popped out. But it *must* be here somewhere. It *has* to be. Just stand there a minute, until we find it. For God's sake, *don't move!*'

'I wasn't going to.' Kay lounged against the door jamb and surveyed the scene. It was a shame, she thought, that photography had ousted the genre painting in this century. A modern Hogarth, or Thomas Savage, might have painted volumes into such topical scenes as 'The Missing Contact Lens'. There could also be that familiar scene of a group of bedraggled people huddled together in the rain, clutching an improbable selection of valuables, whilst staring across the street at police and firemen plunging into the building they had just vacated, and entitled 'Bomb Scare'. Certainly, the twentieth century offered as much scope as the eighteenth. If only there were someone to record it properly – or improperly – it would knock 'Marriage à la Mode' into a cocked hat.

'I told him I'd be useless – ' Marjorie spoke from the comfort of an armchair where she was curled up like a cat, watching the contortions of those crawling across the carpet with a cat's remote amusement.

Sylvia straightened briefly and gave Marjorie a look very reminiscent of her son's.

'Don't stop!' Jeremy applied the spur. 'It's right here somewhere. Oh, God! – you *did* remember the insurance premiums, didn't you?'

'I *think* so.' Sylvia dropped back on to all fours with a guilty alacrity that betrayed her uncertainty. 'I'm sure – almost sure – I did.'

'Oh God!' Jeremy began beating at the carpet, raising tiny puffs of dust. 'Can't you even remember that?' His nose was only inches from the carpet. He sneezed, and clutched desperately at his other eye, seemingly only slightly reassured to find that lens still in place.

Candy and Nick crawled gingerly along the outskirts of the room, leaving the centre of the ring free for the main combatants.

'I can't remember everything!' Sylvia snapped. 'And they are *your* lenses. If you aren't going to pay attention – '

'Here it is!' Jeremy squatted back on his haunches, raising a triumphant finger aloft. 'I've found it!' He pushed the heel of one hand against his eyebrow, distorting his eye socket in a way that made both Marjorie and Kay look away hastily.

'Wash it first!' Sylvia shrieked.

'I was going to!' Jeremy dropped his hand quickly and lurched to his feet. 'Do stop shouting. I don't see why you can't be calm about these things. You *know* my nerves aren't what they ought to be.'

He halted in the doorway, appealing to Kay. 'No one understands the tremendous pressure I'm under at work all day. And then I come home and there's no peace here any more. I can't go on like this. I'm heading for a nervous breakdown!' He dashed down the hallway, muttering to himself.

'I suppose he *is* all right?' Kay looked after him uneasily, before going into the room and sitting down.

'Of course he is,' Sylvia said. 'He really thrives on chaos. He'd die of boredom if he ever got that peace and quiet he's always moaning about.'

'Small chance of that happening *here!*' Jeremy was back in the room already, impelled either by his nervous energy or his fear of missing something. 'Let me get you a drink, Kay. Crispian not with you?'

'He has to cover a recital at the Wigmore Hall tonight,' Kay said. 'He sent his best wishes.'

'Pretty soft,' Jeremy sighed. 'Why didn't *I* opt for being a music critic instead of an advertising genius? No crises, no hysterical clients, no *Sturm und Drang*. That must be the life!'

'It might be, if you weren't tone deaf.' Sylvia had little patience with life's might-have-beens. One gathered that the castles in the air she had been offered for habitation during her early married days had left her ill-disposed to those flights of fancy which the advertising agency had harnessed so profitably.

Kay wondered if it would cheer her to know Crispian also had moments of bemoaning a fate that left him stranded in an aisle seat while Jeremy was 'Making a fortune, simply by juggling meaningless words. The more meaningless the better – and you've got a prize-winning advertising slogan. Set it to even more meaningless chords and notes – and you've got a hit song. Why couldn't I have done that? Why did *I* have to opt for intellectual honesty?' ('You'd hate it, you know you would.') 'Hah! Just try me! Deposit Jeremy's monthly salary cheque in my account and watch me become the perfect intellectual whore – laughing all the way to the bank!'

No, Sylvia would not be interested in, or comforted by, the realization that other women had problems, other men had qualms. If such a truth were to get through to her, she would view it with pained and incredulous disdain. It was one of the things Sylvia did not really want to know.

Perhaps it was the secret of the way men paced each other to success in a way women had not yet learned to do. Women forgave themselves – if not each other – too easily. There was none of the gnawing secret constant measuring of themselves against the accomplishments of someone just ahead of them. Men didn't forgive themselves another's success. Particularly not another who was in the same chronological and intellectual group as themselves. They fought covertly to equal, if not exceed, it. Often they succeeded. It appeared that Crispian and Jeremy were locked in this unadmitted mortal combat now – although both of them would deny it indignantly, if charged with it.

The doorbell cut sharply through her musing. As Sylvia dashed – a little too eagerly – to answer it, Kay belatedly realized that there had been a curious silence in the room for some time. That, in itself, was unusual enough to sharpen her alertness.

She looked around the room, sipping at the drink Jeremy had placed on the sofa table beside her. Marjorie had not lowered her feet to the floor now that it was no longer the scene of an intensive search, but sat with legs still curled under her and a distant smile.

Candice and Nick had resumed their seats – or, rather, seat. Candy occupied an armchair, while Nick lounged on the arm, leaning against the back, one arm outflung to brace himself. They had not looked at each other directly for quite a while.

Jeremy, having dispensed drinks, remained behind the bar as though it were a friendly foxhole. He seemed in no hurry to take part in any conversation after his earlier outburst. Kay wondered how many tranquillizers he had taken during the course of the day. He was mixing them with gin again and it looked as though it might be another early evening.

'We're all here now.' Sylvia bustled Alice and Arthur into the room. 'Jeremy, fix them a drink. You didn't – ' she looked at Alice accusingly – 'bring Barnaby along with you?'

'No, we didn't,' Alice said, although the fact was self-evident. 'He was sleeping and we thought he'd be all right. We can't stay long,' she added thankfully.

'And *you* left Emma home?' The accusation turned against Kay.

'She's all ready for bed and watching television. Crispian will pop her into bed just before he leaves. But I'll have to get back early myself.'

'Barnaby wanted to watch that television programme.' Alice turned to her eagerly. 'I wasn't sure whether we ought to let him or not, but fortunately he fell asleep and that settled that. We were wondering, though, whether we ought to let him stay up later now that he's nine. What do you think?' Alice and Arthur were so determined not to be the sort of doting grandparents who spoiled their only grandchild that Barnaby was in danger of losing out. However, one saw their point. Norman, their only son, was an airline pilot on the international routes and, since his marriage had broken up, Alice and Arthur found themselves in custody of Barnaby more often than even the most doting of grandparents might wish.

'Well, I think – ' Kay began.

'*I* think you're both mad,' Sylvia cut in over her. 'You wouldn't catch *me* leaving Rupert alone in the house, the way things are now.'

'Oh, I say!' Jeremy looked pained. 'They're only squatters, you know, not kidnappers.'

'And they seem to have quite enough children of their own,' Kay put in.

'*Only* squatters!' Sylvia snapped. 'So *that's* your opinion! And suppose it were *our* house they were squatting in?'

'But they aren't – '

'Tell us, dear.' Alice moved in adroitly with diversionary tactics. 'What have you heard from the Norrises? What do they have to say about it all?'

'I haven't heard from them yet.' The admission narrowed Sylvia's eyes, pinched her face and tightened her lips; abruptly she aged twenty years before their eyes. 'But perhaps – ' she took a deep breath, looking on the bright side, and her face returned to normal – 'perhaps they're flying back to deal with it as soon as possible. They may be on the way now.'

'I doubt it,' Marjorie said. 'There's a new Hilton Hotel opening somewhere in the Third World this week. They've probably been flown to the festivities there.'

There was a pause while the others digested this information. The Norrises were travel writers and constantly being spun off to glamorous places at no expense to themselves by optimistic entrepreneurs hoping for free publicity.

'You *knew* that – ' Sylvia's face pinched again – 'and you let me send that Night Letter?'

'It might have reached them.' Marjorie shrugged. 'If not, they'll find it when they get back.'

'*If* they return to that house. They might decide to fly on to their place in Switzerland. Or the flat they keep in New York – '

'Or even here,' Marjorie said mischieviously. 'Wouldn't that be an interesting homecoming for them?'

'I don't think that's funny.' Sylvia stated the obvious flatly.

'Nor do I.' Alice sent Marjorie a glance of prim reproof. 'Those of us with youngsters to look after must take a more serious view of these matters. Mustn't we?' She appealed to Kay.

'I think you're all taking much too serious a view of the whole situation.' Unexpectedly, Jeremy came to the defence. 'People like that come and go. They'll stay here a few weeks and then get bored, or the sink will get stopped up, or something, and they'll move on someplace else.'

'The sink will get stopped up!' Sylvia pounced instantly on the weakest point in his argument. 'Or the toilet will overflow, or the lights will fuse, or the stove catch fire! That's it exactly! Can't you see? These people have no respect for anyone else's property – they don't *care*. As soon as they've made the place unliveable, they'll move on somewhere else. And they'll get away with it because people like you shrug your shoulders and think it doesn't matter – because it's not *your* house they've taken over!'

'Oh, I say – ' Jeremy bleated.

'Why should *you* care? *You're* all right!'

Jeremy finished his drink at a gulp and poured another. He did not look all right. He looked as though he wondered what he had done to bring this fury storming down on his head.

Sylvia had never gone in for causes before. Kay wondered whether there had been a recent marital crisis, or whether Sylvia simply felt threatened by this situation in a way that she had never been threatened by any other social phenomenon. Perhaps it was that no other had struck so close to her before. The squatters had invaded her home territory, stepped into her light and their shadows were stretching across her little world, frightening her. And people who were frightened enough could fight back with a savagery which startled those who thought they knew them best.

'And what about *you*?' Sylvia rounded on Kay suddenly. 'You're off on holiday soon, aren't you? Suppose you come back and find *your* house taken over – ?'

'Now you're just being an alarmist,' Marjorie intervened coolly. 'Kay's position is completely different from that of the Norrises. Her house is her main – her only – abode and squatters wouldn't bother to try taking it over. They'd know that the law would act immediately in her favour.'

Kay had been trying not to think of her impending holiday, but Marjorie was right. Squatters would find it too much trouble to occupy a house for such a short time. The Norrises, on the other hand, would be away indefinitely and even if they returned and got a Court Order, it could still take months to evict their squatters.

'I'm sure it will be all right,' Kay said feebly.

'Besides,' Alice said. 'We'll all keep an eye on Kay's house. No one could move in with all of us keeping watch.'

'It's a pity someone didn't keep watch for the Norrises,' Sylvia said.

'That's unfair,' Jeremy protested. 'How could any of us have expected a thing like that to happen? If anyone had known squatters were on the prowl in this area, of course they'd have kept a look out for them.'

'We know now,' Sylvia said. 'And I think we should be on our guard every minute. Most especially, I don't think anyone ought to go away on holiday and leave their house empty!'

Kay tried to picture Crispian's reaction if she cancelled their holiday because of Sylvia's attitude.

Jeremy stared at Sylvia with a wary, uncomprehending

expression. It was obvious that he wanted to say something soothing, equally obvious that he had no idea what might be soothing to this Amazon warrior who had suddenly appeared by his shrinking side. No wonder he sought inspiration in another deep draught from his glass. The next Client Presentation was going to be child's play by comparison.

Unfortunately, he had to live with Sylvia and not with the clients.

'Look,' he tried brightly. 'Why don't we wait and see if we hear something from the Norrises in the morning? You haven't given them very much time to answer, you know.'

'I'll vote for that.' Nick was already on his feet, pushing Candy towards the door. An ambitious young man on the fringes of the advertising world ought not to be witness to the nervous collapse of an overtired head of one of the leading agencies.

'That sounds logical to me.' Arthur pulled Alice to her feet and started for the door. Although retired, Arthur was basically a Company Man – any Company. Without the one which had signed his salary cheque for so many years, he would settle for the one which seemed to wield the maximum power in terms of social approval.

'There *isn't* much point in staying, since there's nothing we can do.' Kay moved towards the door herself, suddenly anxious to be sure that Emma was safe and asleep. There hadn't been much point in coming, since any action against the squatters would have to be initiated by the owners of the occupied dwelling.

'But can't we *talk*?' Sylvia wailed, seeing her audience escaping. Marjorie had already gained the door and disappeared.

'Emma,' Kay pleaded cravenly. 'I think you're right. She *shouldn't* be left alone.'

Although, really, it was Sylvia who did not wish to be

left alone. What they were all there for was to buttress Sylvia's own sense of insecurity. But surely Jeremy ought to do that?

'If you feel that way –' Jeremy sped the parting guests, obviously feeling no sense of loss. 'We mustn't keep you.' He poured himself another drink, ignoring Sylvia's poisonous gaze.

CHAPTER V

Emma, of course, was sound asleep and perfectly safe.

Kay prepared for bed and propped herself up against the pillows to read until Crispian returned. It was later than usual when she heard the front door open and his steps ascending the stairs.

'How was the new contralto?' she called out cheerily.

'Like a cow with her throat cut.' He appeared briefly in the doorway, glowering.

'Well, *that* ought to have made an interesting column.'

'It ought.' He snarled at her dispassionately, his anger obviously directed against himself. 'Except that the first one to leap to her feet shouting '*Encore*' was the Chairman's wife.'

'We always knew she hadn't any taste.'

'The second one on his feet,' Crispian said, 'was the Chairman himself. And I saw the bouquet they sent up – they'd signed their names on one of the newspaper's cards.'

'Oh dear.' Kay tried to be properly sympathetic, but was already wishing she hadn't bothered to wait up. 'Then she'll be expecting a good review, won't she?'

'So will they.'

'I trust – ' Kay did not quite dare to make it a question, but the mortgage, the rates demand and the repairs needed by the car were uppermost in her mind. 'I trust you tempered the wind to the shorn lambs.'

'Oh, I was polite.' His tone was savage with the realization of his responsibilities. 'I was restrained. I didn't go so far as to give her a *rave* review, but I was temperate. Anyone who wants to read between the lines –

'Anyway, let's look on the bright side. Maybe war will

break out overnight and the paper will spike the review.'
He turned and went down the hall to his study.

In the minutes between turning out the light and actually drifting off to sleep, Kay heard the moody clacking of his typewriter. She wondered if he were working on his Sunday piece, but decided it was more likely that he was again reworking Act I of the play that was going to lift them out of the rat race and on to the pinnacle where their only monetary concern would be which tax haven to choose. If he ever managed to finish it, perhaps it would.

However, he used it as a bulwark against his desperate moments which, since he was of fairly equable temperament, did not occur often enough to allow much progress. If she were a different sort of woman – more scheming or ambitious – probably she could engineer a state of emotional chaos around the house which would keep him glued to his typewriter. But her temperament was too equable, as well. (Would Sylvia have allowed Jeremy to come home and put his feet up with the paper and television if she thought a little judicious nagging might spur him to fresh heights?)

Kay was still smiling at the thought when she fell asleep to the sound of sporadic typing.

She let Crispian sleep late the next day, dispatching Emma to school as quietly as possible under the supervision of a pensive Sylvia and a sulking Rupert. (What new dramas had enlivened *their* breakfast table?)

She then looked in at Crispian, who was still sleeping. A quick glance into the study showed, more ominously, that every last scrap of paper had been tidied away. She knew from experience that this meant nothing new had been accomplished on the play. (New scenes were left proudly beside the typewriter for re-reading the next day.)

The morning was moving on and Crispian showed no

sign of stirring. She would have time to get to the shops before it was necessary to wake him for the day's assignment: the matinee of an Australian string quartet at an ominously obscure venue. This, too, was guaranteed to depress him. ('Why don't they send the kangaroos?')

So, brunch rather than breakfast. And plenty of time to get the day's errands out of the way. She collected her shopping-bag, purse and library books and let herself out quietly, closing the door silently behind her. Perhaps, if the Quartet were depressing enough, Crispian might get back to work on the play tonight.

She was queuing at the greengrocer's when she became aware of a new figure on the horizon. It sailed down the street, attended on both sides by smaller figures, like an ocean liner surrounded by tugs. It took only a moment to realize that she recognized the tugs: they were Emma's new friends. Which must mean that the massive lady they were nudging towards a berth in the sweet shop was one of the adult squatters in the Norris house. Most probably their mother, masquerading as everybody's mother – the Earth Mother incarnate, flowing robes and all – or a woman who hoped to resemble a reasonable facsimile thereof.

Unfortunately for the little tugboats, the sweet shop was on the far side of the greengrocer's and they had to pass Kay to reach it. Intent on their destination, they did not notice her until she greeted them.

'Good morning, Poppy, Jasmine – ' What *was* the other name? Oh yes. 'Heather – '

The Earth Mother halted abruptly, resisting the efforts of her convoy to steer her past this uncharted reef. 'Good morning.' She looked at Kay hopefully. 'Say good morning, girls.'

'Good morning.' Poppy muttered it sullenly, Jasmine with her usual sunny smile, and the baby with an incoherent murmur, which could have been 'Go to hell' – although that was the message flashing from Poppy's eyes.

'We've got to get some chocolate for Wade.' Poppy tried to keep the Earth Mother moving, but might as well have been nudging Gibraltar. The woman stood rooted, beaming vaguely but expectantly at Kay.

'I'm Emma's mother.' Kay introduced herself in the manner most calculated to achieve recognition.

'Oh yes.' The vagueness cleared slightly, probably as much as it ever did, and a hint of enthusiasm crept into the voice. 'We think Emma's great – she's such a *together* kid.'

'Isn't she?' Kay hoped her smile was warm enough almost as much as she hoped that she was interpreting 'together' correctly. 'She's always been a self-sufficient child.'

'That's what I want to teach mine to be,' the Earth Mother confided. 'Oh, excuse me – I'm Elf. Elfrida, really, but all my friends call me Elf.'

It was a nickname that must have started a long time ago, presumably when the lady was more sylphlike than she was now.

'And I'm Kay,' Kay said quickly, lest her private thoughts show through. She debated adding her surname, but first names seemed to be the order of the day.

The children were eyeing them mistrustfully, as though they were a pair of unreliable mongrels who had stopped to sniff at each other and might begin to fight at any moment. Kay smiled at them again, but only Jasmine seemed unconcerned enough to smile back. Poppy stood braced for fight or flight.

Kay transferred her smile to Elf, who seemed serenely unaware of any undercurrents.

'I'm so glad they get on so well with Emma,' Elf said. 'That's why I wanted to move to a nice neighbourhood like this. It's time they met a better class of people and learned how to live properly.'

Kay felt her smile becoming strained.

'I think it's so important for a mother to provide the best environment she can for her children,' Elf went on confidingly. 'It's especially important with a one-parent family. The responsibility is so much greater.'

Kay swept her gaze over the children, each so patently by a different father, and bit back a retort to the effect that she thought the responsibility should have started long before this. She tried to keep smiling.

Perhaps Poppy caught the thought; her face darkened and she began pushing against her mother as though to dislodge her and set her moving away.

'Don't be impatient, Poppy.' Elf patted the tousled head. 'It's nice to stop and pass the time of day with your neighbours.

'She's such a funny kid.' Elf spoke over the child's head to Kay. 'You wouldn't believe the funny ideas she has. They all have. Do you know? – she makes them wash every night. And they *do* it.' She shook her head wonderingly. 'When I was a kid, my greatest ambition was never to have to wash again.'

You're very fortunate. It's not given to everyone to realize their childhood ambitions. Kay tried not to look at the grubby feet protruding over the edges of the well-worn sandals. She looked up hastily and encountered Poppy's hostile gaze.

'Your order – ?'

'Oh, I'm sorry – ' While they had been talking, the queue ahead of Kay had been dealt with. 'A pound of tomatoes, please.' She gave Elf an apologetic nod and turned to the greengrocer, determined to keep occupied with him until Elf was discouraged. 'And a pound of green beans . . . two pounds of onions . . .'

When she finally looked up, after overbuying heavily, Elf had disappeared.

Crispian was moodily drinking re-heated coffee and eating cheese and crackers when she arrived home.

'Why didn't you make fresh coffee?'

Crispian shrugged, very much in one of his martyred moods. She knew that he hadn't been looking forward to the afternoon's assignment, but he needn't begin brooding about it so early. Or was it still last night's brooding carried over?

'I've just met our new neighbours.' Kay offered a distraction. 'Shopping.'

'I suppose they have to eat, too.' He was monumentally uninterested, too wrapped up in his own concerns. He had taken out his pocket diary and was checking his engagements for the rest of the week. They did not appear to cheer him. He shook his head, muttering.

Kay glanced at the clock, sighed, and began preparing lunch. Perhaps Crispian would be more interested in the subject this evening. He would be home late, since he would return to the newspaper office to write his review – which would inevitably lead to going on to a pub with a few of his friends for a drink before they caught their trains home.

Which was all right with her, provided that that was as far as it went. Unfortunately, all too often when he and his cronies were feeling especially impoverished or hard done by, the talk turned to money-making schemes of the most improbable get-rich-quick variety. There had been the plan to go battery-chicken-farming on a farm one of them claimed had been left to him by an elderly uncle – until they'd discovered, when investigating in the sober light of day several days later, that the 'farm' was an end-of-terrace house with large yard on the outskirts of Croydon and the uncle, in any case, was not dead and unlikely to oblige his hopeful nephew for another decade or two.

Then there had been the plan to form a syndicate and buy a race horse – which would, of course, turn out to be a prize-winning champion. This idea had died of natural attrition once they had reckoned the upkeep and maintenance costs of a healthy, hungry colt during the long training period before he was ready to be entered in his first race.

Crispian muttered again and Kay eyed him with foreboding. He was in just the mood to get enthusiastic over another wildcat scheme. She could only hope that he did not encounter a colleague who was hatching one.

CHAPTER VI

It was a good afternoon, Kay decided, to work in the front garden. Less obvious than actually calling Sylvia to tell her about the morning's encounter. A few minutes weeding the herbaceous border was guaranteed to lure one or another of the neighbours out to join her.

She had not anticipated that it might bring Elf out to join her.

But Elf evidently felt that their morning meeting had been as good as a formal introduction. More sinisterly, she also evidently felt that she had a right to behave as though she were an ordinary neighbour, like all the rest, as though she actually belonged in the neighbourhood.

Kay watched, with a faint sense of panic, as Elf appeared in the doorway and waved. Where was Marjorie? She glanced instinctively at Marjorie's blank unhelpful windows, feeling that only a trained sociologist could be expected to cope with the situation.

But just as Elf was about to close the door behind her, she paused and glanced down to the entrance of the Crescent. Her face changed. So, apparently, did her mind. She waved again at Kay and retreated hastily back into the Norris house, closing the front door silently behind her – as though she wished to avoid attracting any attention.

Kay straightened and looked curiously down the street to see what could have caused such an about-face.

But she saw only Norman – Alice and Arthur's airline pilot son – striding complacently along, evidently home on a few days' leave.

'Nice day,' he greeted her.

'Yes, lovely,' she agreed abstractedly. He was carrying,

as usual, a flight bag. Was that what had disturbed Elf? She could have identified the regulars in the Crescent by this time, but the sight of a stranger carrying a flight bag might well have unnerved her. Perhaps she thought it was Mr Norris returning home to stake his claim and begin legal action.

'Having a few days off?' Kay asked, her gaze sliding past him to the Norris front windows, where every curtain twitched. Were they mounting guard against the threatened invasion over there?

'Not before time.' He grinned at her easily but, beneath the heavy tan acquired in some exotic clime, his face was drawn. 'As soon as I catch up on some sleep, I thought I'd take Barnaby to the Zoo. His friends, too, if it's all right with you and Sylvia.'

'Perfectly all right,' Kay said. 'I'm sure Emma would love it – and Rupert, too.' Poor Norman saw his son so sporadically that he was uncertain of his ability to entertain him all alone. It was always the same when Barnaby's father was home – a treat for all the other children, as well as Barnaby.

'That's fine then.' He sent a puzzled glance towards the Norris house, unable to understand the sudden fascination it was exerting on Kay. 'How about tomorrow, if the weather holds fine?'

'I'll tell Emma. I know she'll look forward to it.' Kay decided that was all she was going to tell. Let Alice enlighten her son about the scandalous developments in the neighbourhood. She would enjoy a new and receptive audience.

'Is your mother expecting you?' she asked. Usually, Alice mentioned it when her 'star boarder' was due.

'No.' Again the swift glance towards the Norris house – suspicious now, alerted. In a moment, he would ask what was going on around here. 'I got a chance to swap with another pilot for this week and thought it might be a good idea to spend some time with Barnaby.'

'He'll be thrilled to see you.' Why should she doubt his story? Was it because such a thing had never happened before? Or was it that slight twitch at the corner of one eye – not quite a tic, but . . . ?

'I hope so.' Norman suddenly seemed uneasy and anxious to get away. (Had she been staring?) 'I'll ring you later and make arrangements to collect Emma tomorrow.'

'After school,' Kay reminded him. 'Perhaps you could pick up the children there.' If so, that would give her the afternoon free. She might even get to a matinee herself for a change.

'Right.' He moved off with barely concealed eagerness.

Kay gazed after him thoughtfully, then turned back to survey the border. A large shadow moved behind one of the windows in the Norris house and she decided that she had done enough weeding.

She made one or two more gestures towards the border for the benefit of the watching eyes and retreated into the house before Elf could muster enough nerve to come out again and start a conversation. She didn't feel like seeing any more of the squatter family today.

It was, in fact, the best part of a week before anyone saw any of the squatters again. Not even the children came out to play. There were no more visits to the shops. Only streaks of light glimmering around the edges of the curtains at night betrayed that anyone was still in residence.

'What are they *doing* over there?' Sylvia was reaching breaking-point. '*That's* what I want to know.'

'Oh, Sylvia,' Alice said mildly. 'They're probably just quietly getting on with living. What do you think they might be doing?'

'*Anything!*' Sylvia said darkly, her mind obviously filled

with visions of devastation. 'They could be taking the place apart.'

'Not if they want to go on living there,' Alice protested. 'That wouldn't do them any good. They'd want to keep it nice.'

'*If* they know what the word means.' Sylvia had a point. It was only too obvious that the squatters were accustomed to standards of living that wouldn't pass muster amongst people accustomed to more comfortable modes of life.

'I don't really think they'd go around selling off the furniture.' Candy had been listening quietly, but now she volunteered a crumb of comfort.

'Selling furniture!' Sylvia snorted. 'They're probably ripping out the plumbing.'

'Why would they do that?' Candy asked.

'Why would they do anything? It's not their house and they don't care what happens to it.'

'I'm sure the plumbing is safe,' Kay said. 'The children like it. They're enjoying being able to take baths.' Possibly for the first time in their poor benighted little lives.

'How do you know?' Sylvia did not wait for an answer, assuming the information must have come from Emma or some such unreliable source. 'And where *are* the children? That's what I mean. We haven't seen anyone stirring outside that house for a week. What are they *doing*?'

'What do you expect them to do?' Kay's patience snapped. 'Throw a garden party?'

'No, but I'd expect them to go out and do some shopping. Or let the children out to play. They did that when they first arrived.'

'Perhaps they only shop once a week.' Kay offered amends for snapping. 'When I saw them in the High Street last week, it certainly looked as though they were getting enough supplies to last them through a siege.'

'You *saw* them?' Sylvia pounced on the information. 'You saw *her*? You never told me!'

'There was nothing to tell.' Kay had been hoping to avoid just such a confrontation. 'We only exchanged a few words while I was in the queue at the greengrocer's, and then it was my turn to be served. And she went off with the children to continue her own shopping.'

'Shoplifting, more likely.'

'Sylvia!'

'Well, isn't it? You can't tell me that someone who just walks in and takes over someone else's home is going to be fussy about paying for anything she fancies anywhere else.'

Sylvia had a strong case there and the thoughtful silence proved it. Candy refilled their coffee cups, delighted that the occasional morning coffee klatsch was taking place in her house for a change, and offered more Danish pastries.

'I suppose you haven't heard from the Norrises yet?' Alice asked. It was a fairly safe supposition. If she had heard, Sylvia would have let everyone else know.

'Not yet.' Sylvia's lips tightened. 'I'm afraid Marjorie was right – they weren't going back to the West Indies cottage. I've written to their other addresses. One letter or another ought to catch up with them before too long. We should be hearing something soon.'

Unless, of course, the Norrises had holed up quietly somewhere to finish a new book without distractions. Or perhaps were doing something like investigating tramp steamer routes to rarely-visited corners of the world. It was strange that their neighbours had never noticed before quite how often the Norrises were incommunicado.

'There *are* people going in and out of the house.' Candy refilled her own cup and sat down again, glancing around at the others as though unsure of how much she ought to say. 'But it's at night – '

'What?'
'Who?'
'How do you know?'

'I happened to look out of the front window the other night – Tuesday night – ' Candy took what seemed to be the easiest question first, then discovered that it wasn't so easy after all.

'Nick was awfully late. That is – ' She blushed for her gaucherie in worrying about the lateness of a husband in front of all these assured matrons. 'Well, Nick hadn't been feeling well that morning. I was afraid he might be running a temperature, perhaps feeling dizzy – '

'All right!' Sylvia brushed the explanation aside. 'You looked out of the window. What did you *see*?'

'Nothing really. I mean, a shadow . . . a figure . . . a man . . . slipping around to the back door of the Norris house.'

'There you are!' Sylvia said triumphantly. 'What did I tell you? She'll be hanging out a red light next!'

'Oh, Sylvia!' But the protest was half-hearted. There were, after all, those children of widely differing paternity.

'The awful thing is – ' Having started, it seemed that Candy could not stop. They watched her warily, bracing themselves for a revelation already half-suspected.

'It *is* awful, I know. And it was terribly dark. And I was so worried about Nick that I wasn't really paying attention to anything else. But – ' Candy paused and took a deep breath. 'But I thought there was something vaguely *familiar* about him. Oh, not that I actually knew him – but as though he were someone I'd seen about, or passed in the street. A milkman, perhaps – ' She was stumbling ahead too eagerly. 'Or one of the shopkeepers. Someone you only know vaguely, but couldn't identify right away if you met them outside of where you expected to see them.'

'Perhaps she *doesn't* shoplift,' Sylvia said acidly.

'Perhaps *that's* the way she pays her bills.'

'I didn't say it *was* a shopkeeper,' Candy said in consternation. 'I just said it *might* have been. That sort of person. I mean, someone who was somewhere he didn't belong.'

'*That's* a certainty,' Sylvia said.

'Anyway – ' Candy plunged on to make the point that concerned her most. 'Nick turned the corner while I was still watching and came straight home. So it wasn't *Nick*!'

Perhaps she hadn't meant it that way, but it came out like a challenge. There was another thoughtful silence.

'Tuesday night . . .' Kay took up the glove. 'Crispian covered a concert at the Royal Albert Hall, then he went on to the newspaper office to write his review. It was quite late by the time he'd finished and he was lucky to get a taxi all the way home.'

It was a fuller explanation than she would ordinarily have given, and she did not disallow the possibility that she wanted to reassure herself more than anyone else. It was, indeed, lucky that he had taken a taxi; she had been able to hear it stop outside and the unmistakable chugging ticking-over of engine and meter. Stray taxis were not available in the environs of Crozier Crescent and if one of his friends had given him a lift home it would not have been such a satisfactory alibi. It was not unknown for journalists to back up each other's lies.

'Jeremy worked late again,' Sylvia said swiftly. 'They're preparing a Presentation for a new client. He came home absolutely drained, poor sweet. That job is killing him – but I can't make him give it up. He loves it so.'

'Norman was out with his father.' Forthrightly, Alice did not attempt to embroider her information. 'They went on a pub crawl, they told me. That was why I wasn't invited. That, and because I didn't want to leave Barnaby alone. Norman and Arthur were together all evening . . . I think.'

'Nevertheless,' Sylvia said, 'this is a new development. A very unpleasant one. I think we ought to hear what our dear Marjorie has to say about the situation now.'

'It's a shame she couldn't come this morning,' Candy said. 'I invited her, but she had to work.'

Marjorie. They contemplated her for a moment. With a job to go to during the day, and no husband's whereabouts to worry about at night. Lucky Marjorie.

Kay was suddenly very glad that she, Crispian and Emma were taking off for a fortnight's holiday at the end of the week.

By the time they returned, perhaps the situation would have resolved itself.

CHAPTER VII

However, they returned from holiday to find that nothing had changed. Or very little.

The squatter children were on view again. Poppy crouched beside a rose-bush, giving a creditable imitation of the other amateur gardeners of the Crescent, picking the greenfly off of it. Jasmine drifted nearby, occasionally removing a greenfly, but more often just cradling a blossom in her hand and sniffing happily. Heather was propped up against the front steps, from which vantage point she viewed the world as impassively as ever.

Poppy raised her head as their car drove up and scowled. Jasmine beamed at them and waved in greeting. The baby didn't even blink.

It seemed that things were much as they had left them.

And their own house was safe: empty and waiting for them, to Kay's relief. Despite Marjorie's expert assurances, there had still been a few nagging fears. Even though, as Crispian had pointed out, cancelling their holiday could have cost them more, in terms of money, time and energy, than ejecting squatters – if they should find any – upon their return.

Kay had been too exhausted by packing by that time to argue the possible damage that squatters might leave in their wake. She knew what Crispian's answer would have been: 'We have insurance'. But insurance money would not replace objects which had been bought with loving care and treasured for their memories. Nor would any amount of cleaning and painting cover the shadow of defilement that would always, in one's mind, remain over the rooms that had been violated.

But the worry had been unnecessary. The only unpleasantness awaiting them was the pile of bills in the front hall.

Mindful of Emma's listening ears, Crispian turned the word he had in mind into a formless grunt as he bent and swept up the pile of bills. His face was whiter than it had been since he cashed their last travellers' cheque with two days to go before they started back.

Kay met his gaze sympathetically, if a little wryly. What had he expected? He knew that the bills were due. Naturally they were going to arrive, whether or not the addressee were there to receive them.

'I'll deal with these later.' He flicked through them, wincing, and set them down on the table.

'Sufficient unto the day,' Kay agreed. There was all the unpacking ahead of them still, and tomorrow she must get to the laundrette with all the dirty clothes. But, for the moment, it was enough just to be back in her own house again.

The telephone rang before they had finished the unpacking. As might have been expected, it was Sylvia.

'How about coming over for drinks this evening and telling us all about your trip?'

It wasn't a bad idea, although Kay suspected they'd do more listening than talking. She referred the question to Crispian.

'Why not?' He looked at the alternative: the pile of bills waiting to be gone through.

'We'd love to, thanks,' Kay said.

'Bring Emma too,' Sylvia directed. 'Rupert will be delighted to see someone his own age again. I'm afraid he's been getting a bit bored with Barnaby.'

'We'll do that,' Kay said and rang off. The eldest squatter child was about Rupert's age, but obviously Sylvia hadn't lowered her defences enough to permit fraternization. Which would make it awkward when Emma wanted to play with the other children and Rupert was forbidden their company. Kay wondered what stance Alice had decided to take with regard to Barnaby. Probably the same as Sylvia's, since it sounded as though Rupert and Barnaby had been having too much of each other's company these days.

'Haven't you got a lovely tan? Did you have a good time?' The second question was as rhetorical as the first. Sylvia didn't wait for any answers. 'Emma, run upstairs and play with Rupert. Oh – is that for him? How – how nice.' She met Kay's rueful grimace of apology over Emma's head. 'I'm sure he'll love it.'

He probably would. The pottery bull, complete with toreador, was just gruesome enough to delight Rupert and they had not been able to dissuade Emma from buying it out of her own pocket money.

'Come in, come in and have a drink.' Jeremy swayed hospitably in the doorway. 'God – you're looking healthy! I wish *I* could take some time and get away. But there's no rest for the weary.'

'Or the wicked.' Crispian followed him over to the bar and began making himself at home. 'How many new clients have you acquired to swindle while we've been away?'

'Oh, one or two . . . one or two.' Jeremy blinked owlishly, then closed one eye at a time, checking the focus on the farther wall to make sure he hadn't dislodged his contact lenses again. It made him look either very drunk or slightly mad, Kay couldn't decide which. Perhaps a bit of both.

'Well.' Kay turned to Sylvia to give her the opening she was obviously awaiting. 'Have we missed any excitement while we've been away?'

'It's more infuriating than exciting,' Sylvia said. '*They're* still there.'

'I know,' Kay said. 'We saw the children as we drove

up. They seemed to be working in the garden.'

'Oh yes, the children aren't so bad,' Sylvia admitted. 'They always seem to be doing little jobs around the place – especially the eldest one.'

'Poppy,' Kay supplied. It was ridiculous for Sylvia to keep on pretending that she didn't even know their names. 'Poppy, Jasmine and Heather. In that order.'

'Idiotic names,' Sylvia said. 'Why on earth do you suppose that lazy slut chose names like that?'

'Perhaps she's a romantic,' Kay said. 'More probably, she started out as one of the Flower Children and they're – '

'Souvenirs?' Sylvia glanced swiftly over her shoulder to make sure the men weren't paying attention and lowered her voice. 'And they're not the *only* souvenirs. There's a man living over there, too. We've seen him now. He's an *addict!*'

'Addict?' Kay looked at her blankly.

'A Registered Addict. Drug. *You* know. There were a lot of them around a few years ago.'

'Not around here.'

'Well, there is now!' Sylvia nodded with satisfaction. For once, Kay had reacted in the proper way.

Across the room, Crispian looked up suddenly, as though a shock wave had reached him. Kay wondered if Jeremy were breaking the news to him over there.

'How do you know?' Kay was still faintly incredulous. And yet it was all part of the pattern.

'For one thing, he's transferred his "account" to the chemist in the High Street and collects his drugs there. For another, we've seen him now. The weather has been marvellous since you left and he's been sitting outside – staring into space. I suppose that's why they call it "spaced-out".'

'Who's spaced out?' Jeremy brought Sylvia a drink, Crispian carried Kay's.

'We're talking about that drug addict over in the Norris house – the Army deserter.' Sylvia filled them in.

'Army deserter?' Crispian raised an eyebrow. 'Then we'll be having a raid by the Military Police any time now. That will take care of your squatter problem.'

'Oh, not *our* Army,' Sylvia said. 'The American. But I don't think they're interested in him.' Her tone implied that they could not be faulted for that.

'No one is even sure *which* war he deserted from. He isn't very young and he looks as though he's on his last legs. Those sort don't usually last very long. It's *too* bad if he has to die in Crozier Crescent, though.'

'People have to die somewhere,' Jeremy pointed out reasonably.

'It *would* lower the tone of the neighbourhood, I can see,' Crispian said with spurious sympathy.

'Well, it *would*.' Sylvia shot him a suspicious look, ignoring Jeremy. 'And in the Norris house, too.'

'One house is as good as another for that sort of thing.' Jeremy was still determined to be philosophical about it. 'But I think you're kissing him off much too early, old girl. He doesn't look all that bad to me.'

'You're an expert, I suppose?'

'I've seen a few.' Jeremy nodded judiciously. 'When you're dealing with creative staff, you pretty much see everything. And sometimes, after years and years of the stuff, they pull themselves together and snap back into normal life. All the psychologists say so.'

'You've been talking to Marjorie, I suppose?'

'We've exchanged a few words,' Jeremy admitted. 'Not necessarily on that subject. But I've been talking to her, yes.'

'Is that the total over there?' Kay intervened hastily. 'One female adult, one male drug addict adult, and the three children?'

'So far,' Sylvia said.

'Oh, come now.' Jeremy was in an argumentative mood. 'You don't really expect any more are going to join them?'

'Who knows? There's plenty of room,' Sylvia added darkly, 'in the Norris house.'

'Have you heard anything from the Norrises yet?' This time it was Crispian who decided to intervene.

'Not a word.' Sylvia became grim. 'They're obviously off exploring some quaint corner of the world. By the time their post catches up with them, it will be too late.'

'Too late for what?' Jeremy was determined to look on the bright side. 'At least, if the chap is a registered addict, they won't have to sell off the furniture to support his habit.'

'Oh, really!' Sylvia turned her back on her husband in disgust.

'Another drink, old chap?' Jeremy repossessed Crispian's glass and lurched towards the bar.

'Oh, yes.' Sylvia was at the window and suddenly diverted. 'I forgot to tell you. Norman is joining us for drinks, too. Here he comes now.'

'Oh? Is Norman back again?' Automatically, Kay moved to the window.

'Not *back* – ' Sylvia gave her a meaningful glance. '*Still* here. He *says* he's on holiday.'

'Oh?' It was as much encouragement as Sylvia needed. Or Jeremy either, for that matter.

'If you ask me,' Sylvia said, 'he's on leave. Indefinite leave. *Sick* leave.'

'Afraid she's right,' Jeremy chimed in. 'Our Norman is more than slightly the worse for wear these days. If *I* were Personnel Manager at the airlines, I'd have suggested a nice long holiday, too.'

'I did notice – ' Kay gazed through the curtains as the object of their conversation advanced unsuspectingly. 'The last couple of times we saw him – just before we left on holiday – he *did* look a bit nerve-racked.'

'Racked? Wrecked!' Jeremy confirmed cheerfully. 'He's a nervous wreck. He's been getting worse and worse. Pretend you don't notice it,' he added. 'No use making the poor chap any more self-conscious.'

'It's a shame,' Sylvia said. 'He was doing so well in his career.'

'It can't be that bad.' With all those bills waiting for him back at the house, Crispian was a little sensitive on career matters. 'Norman's always been very calm and steady. He has to be, to pilot those planes.'

'*Aye, there's the rub.*' Jeremy nodded. 'Now, you take me. *I'm* a nervous wreck – and who cares? All part of the game. No one is going to worry if their advertising executive is a nervous wreck. The clients simply accept it as their due. But the last thing a paying customer aboard a Jumbo jet wants to see is his pilot with a twitch.'

The doorbell rang and they all jumped guiltily.

'I'll go.' His natural duplicity asserting itself, Jeremy rearranged the lines of his face into a welcoming smile and headed for the door.

They heard his voice raised in greeting and then he was ushering Norman into the room. Kay experienced her second severe shock of the evening.

The incipient twitch at the corner of Norman's eye had flowered into a fully developed tic. There was a distinct tremor in the hand he stretched out to accept the drink from Jeremy. It looked as though the airline had removed him from the pilot's seat just in time.

But . . . wasn't Jeremy also a great deal unsteadier than he had been just before they left on holiday? He was swaying visibly and it was only with difficulty that he managed to transfer the glass to Norman's shaking hand from his own shaking hand. Standing there, side by side, they looked like the sort of advertising illustration that used to be subtitled: 'Don't Let This Happen To You!'

Kay blinked and looked away. Was she imagining

things? Or did everyone just look worse because she was so newly returned from a refreshing holiday and had not yet re-oriented herself to the appearance of those who had not been on holiday?

But Norman was supposed to be having his holiday now. It didn't seem to be doing him any good.

Inadvertently, Kay met Crispian's worried gaze and knew that it was not just her imagination.

They had two old neighbours on the verge of acute nervous breakdowns. And a new neighbour who was a drug addict waiting for death to overtake him.

CHAPTER VIII

Kay was working at the back of the house later in the week when she heard the sudden ecstatic screams of the squatter children. Because it was so unusual for them to be noisy, she hurried to a window to see what was happening.

But there was nothing to be seen. A toy lay beside the front steps, as though abandoned hastily. That, too, was unusual. The squatter children had never been trusting enough to leave their few toys scattered around the way normal children did. Perhaps bitter experience with others of their ilk had taught them not to.

The Norris front door hung ajar, still quivering with the force of someone's passage. Even as she watched, it closed slowly and finally, shutting out the rest of the world.

Feeling rebuked, Kay turned away from the window and went back to her work, still conscious of a nagging curiosity. Sooner or later, she knew, someone would be able to tell her what had just happened. The Crescent was never so quiet and deserted as it might seem to an outsider just walking past.

She had not long to wait. Sylvia was on the telephone before the breakfast dishes were finished.

'She has *another* man over there now.' Sylvia skipped the preliminaries and went straight to the main event. 'He came about half an hour ago, and – ' Sylvia's voice rose hysterically – '*this* one is black!'

'Oh,' Kay said. Given the hue of little Jasmine, it was difficult to see just why this development should have come as such a shocking revelation to Sylvia.

'Did you hear what I said?' Once again, her reaction

had not been satisfactory. 'I said *black*.'

'I heard you,' Kay said. 'I just don't know what you expect me to do about it.'

There was a suspicious silence, then Sylvia asked abruptly, 'Is Marjorie there with you?'

'No,' Kay said. 'I'm alone. Why?'

'I just thought you sounded like her suddenly. So – so *clinical*. She might have been prompting you from the background.'

'I *am* capable of carrying on a conversation without Marjorie's advice.' Evidently she sounded sufficiently offended for Sylvia to apologize.

'I'm sorry. I just thought – I didn't mean – ' It seemed that apologies could go no further. Sylvia's voice ran down and halted.

It was with relief that Kay heard the sudden peal of the doorbell.

'I'm sorry, Sylvia,' she said. 'I've got to go. There's someone at the door.' She hung up before Sylvia could answer.

Alice rushed past her as though pursued by demons when she opened the front door. The onrush carried Alice halfway down the hall before she stopped abruptly and turned back, panting, her eyes wild and beseeching.

'I know,' Kay said. 'I've just heard. He's black.'

Alice nodded frantically, trying to fan herself into composure with one hand while the other hand groped for the support of the wall.

'I left Barnaby . . . with Arthur,' Alice panted. 'Norman isn't . . . feeling very well.' A comment that could cover anything from a hangover to breaking up the furniture in his bedroom. 'Where's Emma?'

'At the Victoria and Albert Museum,' Kay answered calmly. 'Crispian had the day off and decided to give her an outing.'

'What a pity I didn't know that.' Alice was momentarily

sidetracked. 'Barnaby loves the V & A and he hasn't been there in ages.'

Kay refrained from pointing out that not every father felt the need to move in convoy with his own child. Crispian and Emma were on comfortable enough terms to enjoy the luxury of a day in each other's company without the intrusion of any other personalities.

'I haven't much time, Alice. I'm meeting Crispian and Emma in town. We're going out to lunch.' It wasn't quite a lie – she had just shortened the time span. 'I'll have to be leaving soon to meet them.'

'Yes, of course,' Alice said, flustered. 'I didn't intend to stay. I just came to ask – '

'I've heard,' Kay said. 'Sylvia called me.'

'And me.'

'Yes, I thought she'd be having a busy morning on the telephone.'

'Well, you can't blame her,' Alice defended. 'Not really. She's concerned about the situation. She has Rupert to consider. I'm worried myself – for Barnaby's sake. And so ought you to be – for Emma, if not for yourself.'

'Emma is living in a world in which she's going to have to mix with a lot of different people as she grows older. I don't feel it can do her a great deal of harm to start sooner rather than later.'

'You sound like Marjorie.' Again, there was a subtle accusation in the statement.

'Perhaps you ought to have a little talk with Marjorie yourself – you and Sylvia.'

'I didn't mean to disturb you when you were getting ready to go out,' Alice said stiffly. 'I'll be getting along.'

'I'm sorry.' Kay was contrite, but not enough to attempt to stop her. 'Why don't you come round for coffee in the morning?' She walked to the front door with Alice.

'I'll let you know,' Alice said distantly.

As Kay opened the door, she saw Candy hurrying past

with a strained expression. Poor Candy and Nick had taken on more than they bargained for when they bought the old Elwood house. It must have seemed such a nice quiet *safe* neighbourhood for first-time buyers and they couldn't have moved into more of a hornets' nest if they had tried.

Kay waved, but Candy did not appear to notice.

'Candy, wait a minute – ' Alice called and hurried towards her.

Candy stopped reluctantly, looking as though she would have liked to avoid the encounter. But Candy was usually only too ready to be friendly. Was the new atmosphere beginning to get her down?

Feeling that they all deserved an afternoon unencumbered by the cares of Crozier Crescent, Kay did not mention the new squatter. So they were unprepared to find the windows of the Norris house wide open upon their return. There were no lights showing, but the curtains were blowing in the breeze and seemed to ripple in time to the gusts of melody floating out from the house.

'I didn't know they were musical.' Crispian paused, caught by the rich deep voice floating effortlessly across the Crescent.

'. . . *She asked me to marry,*
  '*Took hold of my hand,*
  '*And said, "You're a stranger*
  '*"And in a strange land"* . . .'

'Haven't heard that one in years,' Crispian said. 'Old American folksong. Of course, the drug addict is American, isn't he?'

'. . . *"My father's a Chieftain,*
  '*"A ruler he be,*
  '*"I'm his only daughter . . .*
  '*"MY NAME IS MO-HEE"* . . .'

A chorus of children's voices joined in on the line and

burst into self-congratulatory laughter. Over them rolled a deeper richer laughter.

'It's not a record!' Crispian sounded shocked by the realization. 'Do you mean to say that drug addict can sing like that? What a waste!'

'Don't be silly,' Emma said. 'Wade can't sing. Wade can't do *anything*.' Her nose wrinkled scornfully. 'He just sits there and pushes needles into himself.'

There was no use asking Emma how she knew. It would only put her on the defensive again. Although they had been home for less than a week, it would be a fair bet that Emma knew more of what was going on in the neighbourhood than they did.

Besides, it was quite possible that Emma had known before they went on holiday. The children had been in and out of the Norris house unbeknownst for some time before the adults had realized anything was going on. How much else had she learned? That offhand remark about needles had been unpleasantly graphic.

Kay and Crispian met each other's eyes reflectively and urged Emma forward again. They entered their own house in silence, the deep glorious voice following them across the Crescent.

'. . . *I answered and told her*
'*It never could be* . . .'

The front door closed behind them, cutting off all outside sounds. Crispian looked thoughtful.

'Then who *is* singing over there?' he asked.

'I didn't have a chance to tell you earlier – ' Kay nodded her head towards Emma meaningfully. 'But we seem to have a new neighbour. I haven't seen him yet myself, but I understand another man moved in over there this morning.'

'He hasn't moved in,' Emma corrected unconcernedly. 'He's only visiting.'

'Who is?' Kay asked, her worst fears confirmed. Emma *did* know everything that was going on.

'The one who's singing,' Emma said. 'I expect that's Sinbad. Sinbad – come home from the sea.'

CHAPTER IX

All the next morning, Crispian was abstracted. He kept pacing about the house, his steps frequently carrying him past the windows, where he always paused, peering out intently from behind the curtains.

'For heaven's sake,' Kay protested. 'You're getting as bad as Sylvia!'

'So long as I don't get as bad as Jeremy . . .' Crispian looked at his watch again.

Emma hopped down the stairs on one foot, not holding on to the banister. '*Why* can't I go out to play?' she demanded.

'No one else is out playing.' Kay avoided a direct answer.

'If *I* go out, then some of the others will,' Emma said practically.

'Later.' Kay knew it was true. Once Sylvia and Alice saw Emma outside, they would probably allow Rupert and Barnaby out. 'After you've tidied your room.' It was always a safe assumption that Emma's room was not in any state a parent would consider satisfactory.

With a martyred sigh, Emma turned slowly and began hopping back up the stairs, still not holding on. Kay caught her breath as Emma seemed to overbalance dangerously and then righted herself. It was all part of the parent-child war of nerves. The trouble was that parental nerves were older and had less elasticity, as well as being stretched in other directions by outside events.

Crispian took another turn around the room and halted once more by a window. 'Perhaps it might be a good idea to let her go out,' he said. 'Get some fresh air, see her little friends – '

'Crispian.' Kay was suddenly, sharply suspicious. 'What are you up to?'

Crispian took one more look out of the window, another glance at his watch, and then raised his eyes above and beyond her in a gaze of improbable innocence. 'I think I'll take the dog for a walk,' he murmured.

'We don't have a dog,' Emma pointed out. Silent and unnoticed, she had crept back into their company. 'If we had a dog, you could take it for a walk.' She was always ready to discuss a reasonable proposition. '*Why* don't we get a dog?'

Now look what you've started.

Crispian flinched before the wifely message, but held his ground. 'Don't wait lunch. I'll pick up a snack along the way.'

'I suppose that means you're going to the pub,' Emma translated with unerring accuracy. 'Why can't I come and have squash and crisps outside?'

'Why don't you stop asking questions?' For a moment, Crispian descended to her level before remembering he was supposed to be the all-wise adult. 'I can't take you along. He fell back on another unfortunate cliché. 'I have to see a man about a dog.'

'You mean we're getting one?' Emma's face was radiant. 'What kind? When will we get it? For my birthday? What will I name it? I'll take care of it, truly I will. I won't let it bother you at all. I promise.'

'I mustn't be late.' Crispian edged towards the door. 'Your mother will explain it to you.' Male chauvinist coward to the core, he slipped away and left Kay to rectify the situation.

'Will it be a puppy?' Emma's eyes were shining; she had forgotten anything else in the world existed. 'Can I choose it? What kind will it be?'

'Have you tidied your room yet?' Kay asked sternly, unable to cope with more complex questions.

'I'll do it now.' Emma flew towards the stairs. 'I'll get it so clean it's shining. Just wait till I tell Rupert!'

Crispian had not returned by the time they finished lunch, so Kay put his salad in the fridge, left a note on the table, and, shamelessly bribing Emma with the promise of a side-trip to the library, swept her off for the afternoon's shopping.

She left Emma to browse in the Children's Section and went upstairs to the Adult Fiction. She bumped into Marjorie rounding the corner from Non-Fiction.

'So you're back,' Marjorie said. 'Have a nice time?'

'Lovely, thanks. It's nice to be home, though.'

'Is it?' Marjorie raised a mildly disbelieving eyebrow. 'I shouldn't think you'll keep that attitude very long.'

'Oh, I know things are still in a turmoil,' Kay said. 'But they'll settle down eventually. Not even Sylvia can stay at such a fever pitch of indignation for ever.'

'I wouldn't be too sure of that. If it's a matter of self-interest, I think Sylvia could do almost anything.'

'I left Emma downstairs while I came up to choose my own books.' Kay changed the subject, tired of the same old problem. What *had* everyone found to talk about before the squatters moved in? And yet she seemed to remember hours of pleasant conversation unshadowed by social issues – at least, not ones directly pertinent.

Marjorie was carrying an armload of books so heavy and of such serious content that they could only be called tomes.

'Don't you ever read fiction?' Kay asked curiously.

'I might if I could find anything worthwhile,' Marjorie said. 'But all that I can see of it simply annoys me. Here in England today, we're in the forefront of the most exciting social changes since the Industrial Revolution – and most of our novelists are paying no attention. They're too busy examining their own entrails and issuing breathless reports to a world they imagine peopled exclusively by their Oxbridge contemporaries. Nothing they have to say bears any relevance to the real world and they bore me rigid.'

'I suppose – ' Kay was very glad that she had not been caught coming away from the shelves, condemned by her choice of fiction. 'I suppose you're so aware of what's going on that it would be boring for you.'

'Isn't it for you? Just look at where we stand today. Some of the most challenging social innovations ever experienced are going on all around us: pop culture, industrial democracy – '

'And squatting?' Sylvia had come up behind them, obviously in her most acid mood.

'That, too.' Marjorie was not prepared to back down. 'It's all part of the changing social order.'

'I thought I'd find you up here.' Sylvia turned to Kay, dismissing Marjorie. 'I saw Emma downstairs when I left Rupert there. It looks as though we've both had the same idea.'

'What idea is that?' Kay asked cautiously. Sylvia was looking at her with too much approval. She knew she had done nothing to deserve it.

'We've found a place to bring the children where we know they won't run into *them*.' She could not resist a sidelong glance at Marjorie. 'They probably don't even know that such things as libraries exist – if they can even read.'

'I hadn't thought of that,' Kay said. 'Emma wanted to get some books, and so did I. That's why we're here.'

'You wouldn't admit it in front of Marjorie, anyway,' Sylvia said. 'You're afraid she'd disapprove.'

'I'd never disapprove of people utilizing libraries – for whatever reason.' Marjorie was looking dangerously thoughtful. 'I think you've made an excellent point. Those children *ought* to have library cards – at least, the older two. I'll speak to Elf about it. Now that they have a fixed address, there shouldn't be any difficulty.'

'But it's not *their* fixed address!' It was impossible to tell whether Sylvia's anguish was at the impending disappearance of what she had considered a safe haven for Rupert, or the idea of anything that might seem to be absorbing the squatters into the life of the community. 'It's the Norrises' fixed address!'

'Hardly fixed,' Marjorie reminded her. 'They haven't lived there for more than six months and they have at least three other addresses all around the world. They've probably bought a new place by now and are living there and that's why you haven't heard from them. Or – ' she twisted the knife delicately – '*have* you heard from them?'

'No,' Sylvia admitted, flushing with annoyance. 'But when I do – '

'*Shhhh!*' Like an explosive charge of pent-up fury, the shushing sound came from two readers and a librarian at the same time and Sylvia's vague threat remained unuttered.

'I suppose we shouldn't stand here talking.' Kay lowered her voice self-consciously. 'I must go and choose my books.'

'I'll wait for you,' Sylvia said. 'We can all walk back together.'

'I'll get mine charged out and go along,' Marjorie said. 'I can't wait.'

Kay would have preferred it the other way around, but knew that she was stuck with Sylvia. Besides, Rupert and Emma would have linked up by now, so she was trapped in any case.

'*Shhhh!*'

Exchanging guilty smiles, they split up to go their various ways. Kay, her mind no longer on the books she wanted, browsed aimlessly, conscious that Sylvia had taken up a waiting position beside the stairs to the

Children's Section. Marjorie waved to them both impartially as she left, happily unconscious of Sylvia's furious glare.

Where did anyone ever get the idea that tiny footsteps pattered? A thundering charge swept up the stairs. The heads of those trying to read snapped up and baleful eyes focused on the head of the stairs. Only in a perfect world would a herd of elephants have lumbered into view.

As it was, Emma and Rupert cleared the top step with a bound and advanced on mothers who, conscious of the disapproval emanating from all sides, were no longer so anxious to claim them.

'Emma's going to get a puppy.' Rupert aired his grievance loudly. 'Why can't I have a puppy?'

'She isn't!' Sylvia looked from Emma to Kay accusingly. 'Is she?'

With a sinking heart, Kay saw the titles of the books Emma clutched so proudly: *How To Choose Your Puppy*, *Caring For Your Puppy* and *Training Your Dog*.

'Why can't I have a dog?' Rupert demanded again.

'*Shhhh!*'

'You're *not* going to give her one?' Sylvia rounded on Kay. 'You *know* the city is no place to bring up a dog.'

'It's all right if it's a small dog – and I don't really want a big one.' Trusting and complacent, Emma gazed at her mother with shining eyes and Kay quailed before her gaze. 'I'm getting one for my birthday.'

'How *could* you?' Sylvia said. 'You *knew* the chain reaction it was bound to have.'

It was unfair. In the first place, it was Crispian's fault. Let *him* talk Emma out of this. In the second place, why *shouldn't* Emma get a puppy for her birthday? She was old enough to take care of one and she had certainly shown an excellent sense of initiative and responsibility by choosing the proper books to study beforehand.

'*Shhhh!*'

'Oh, let's get out of here!' Sylvia snapped.

On the walk home, an armed truce existed between Sylvia and her son, although Kay would not like to have been called upon to decide which one was in a worse sulk.

Emma, sensing that she had somehow made great strides forward in achieving what had become her heart's desire, walked sedately beside Kay, quietly gloating over her books.

As they turned the corner into Crozier Crescent, Sylvia drew in her breath sharply. 'Look at that! They're turning the Crescent into a slum!'

The squatters were out in force. Elf and Poppy were spreading washing over the bushes to dry. A large powerfully-built black man was working in the garden. One could see how beautifully muscled he was, since he wasn't wearing a shirt. A painfully thin pallid man, who must be Wade the addict, slumped on the steps with Heather slumped at his feet, both staring blankly into space. Jasmine, like a bright bronze butterfly, flitted from one to another.

It took Kay a moment to realize the most incongruous thing about the scene before her. Every one of them, except the black man, was wearing a sort of terrycloth turban.

Unperturbed, Emma and Rupert broke away from their stunned mothers and advanced on their playmates.

'I'm going to get a puppy.' Emma went straight to the heart of the matter. Jasmine darted over to her immediately.

'Isn't that nice?' The black man straightened and smiled genially.

'When?' Jasmine demanded, looking around as though expecting to see a puppy frisking at Emma's feet already.

'For my birthday,' Emma said confidently. 'It's going to be a surprise.'

'Always nice to have a surprise for your birthday,' the black man chuckled.

'Oh, won't that be lovely?' Leaving Poppy to struggle on alone with the laundry, Elf drifted over to join them.

'Don't start a conversation!' Sylvia hissed in Kay's ear. 'Ignore them!'

It would be like trying to ignore a force of nature: a hurricane, perhaps; or, more aptly, the slow encroaching spill of boiling lava creeping down the side of a volcano after an eruption.

She tried to wrench her eyes away from the embroidered '*N*' on the pillowcase Poppy was draping across the sturdiest rose-bush.

'They'll be dry in no time, this weather.' The man followed her gaze. 'Much nicer to have them dry out in the clean fresh air, gives them a good smell.'

Now that he mentioned it, there was a distinct odour in the air. Repugnant and faintly familiar . . .

'My mother did that to my head, too.' Rupert pinpointed it before the adults did, looking at the towelling wrapped around Jasmine's head.

'Mine too,' Emma agreed.

'Sorry about that.' Large brown humorous eyes went apologetically from Kay's face to Sylvia's. 'Just a little problem we had. All taken care of now. It won't trouble anyone again.'

Kay hadn't realized she was returning the smile until Sylvia's elbow dug into her ribs sharply.

If Jasmine was a butterfly, Poppy was a moth. She gave a final smoothing twitch to the pillowcase and sidled forward, staring at the books under Emma's arm.

'Rupert – ' Sylvia was tugging at the back of her son's collar. 'Rupert, come along. We can't stand here all day. We have things to do.'

'What things?' Without realizing it, Rupert called his mother's bluff.

'Things,' Sylvia said firmly, giving him a tug that jerked him backwards, nearly overbalancing him. 'Your father will hear about this, if you don't come along promptly and stop arguing.'

'*My* father is getting me a dog,' Emma informed Poppy, in case she had missed the first broadcast of the news. 'I'm going to choose what kind I want and take care of it all by myself.' She flourished the books at Poppy.

Poppy fluttered closer, obviously reluctant to come within the adult sphere, but unable to resist the lure.

'An Afghan is too big.' Emma had opened the book depicting breeds and was surveying an illustration with a proprietorial air. 'It wouldn't do for the city. I wouldn't like a Great Dane, either.' She flipped the pages. They were undoubtedly in for some long long discussions of the finer points of each breed and its drawbacks.

'Mmm.' Poppy's eyes never left the shining pages. She was not envying Emma the promised dog, Kay realized suddenly, she was envying her the books.

'*My* father will get me a dog if I ask him.' It was not easy for Rupert to swagger with Sylvia's hand firmly entwined in his collar, but he nearly managed it.

Jasmine moved closer and slipped her little hand into the large dark chocolate hand. 'Sinbad is *my* father,' she informed them unnecessarily.

At Wade's feet, Heather was galvanized into action. She hurled herself forward and twined around Sinbad's ankles. 'Mine! Mine!' she wailed jealously.

Sylvia's indrawn breath was sharp and distinct.

Poppy fell back against him, taking his other hand in both of her own. 'Sinbad is *all* our fathers,' she said defiantly.

'Really!' Sylvia did not attempt to disguise her reaction.

'Don't knock it, lady.' Sinbad met her eyes with a level hostility that matched her own. 'I may not be your idea of a father figure, but I'm all these kids have got – and don't you forget it!'

Sylvia backed away hastily with Rupert. Kay caught Emma's elbow and drew her back. For once, the children were unresisting, sensing the menace of the changed mood.

'Goodbye for now,' Elf called after them, beaming serenely. 'Why don't you come over for coffee some evening?'

CHAPTER X

'Why *don't* we go over for coffee?' Crispian asked when Kay told him about it later.

Kay laughed and then saw that he was serious. She stopped laughing.

'I mean it,' Crispian said. 'You seem to have established diplomatic relations. They're obviously not going to slink away quietly if we ignore them. I think Marjorie had the best idea – and she's the expert on these things – befriend them. Why shouldn't we?'

'Sylvia would never speak to us again,' Kay said.

'Best possible argument in favour. Unfortunately, it's specious. You know Sylvia would forgive us anything in exchange for a first-hand report on what the inside of the house looks like now. So long as she didn't have to sully her own self-image by setting foot inside it herself.'

It was true. In fact, Kay was curious herself to know the state of the Norris furniture and the extent of any depredations.

'Come on. Why hesitate?' Crispian was on his feet, prowling towards the windows.

'Not tonight,' Kay said firmly. 'The way we left them this afternoon wasn't very diplomatic.'

'That was Sylvia's fault,' Crispian pointed out. 'Not yours.'

'Still,' Kay said, 'I think we ought to allow a little time for the memory to fade.'

'You may be right.' Crispian shrugged, his attention caught by something outside. He pulled aside the curtain, waved a signal and turned back into the room.

'Nick and Candy are going down to the pub,' he said.

'I think I'll go along. You don't want to leave Emma, do you?'

'No.' Even if she had, the wording of the question would have precluded it.

'I won't be too long.' He was opening the front door as he spoke. It closed behind him on the final word.

Kay had scarcely time to begin to examine her feelings – she suspected she was annoyed – before the doorbell rang.

'I decided to come back and stay with you.' Candy stood on the step. 'Crispian will keep Nick company at the pub and they'll be happier without me along.'

'Come in.' Kay opened the door wider. 'Would you like a cup of tea, or shall we have a drink ourselves?'

'I don't care.' Candy moved out of the shadows and Kay saw her distraught face. 'I just want someone to talk to.'

'I see.' Kay felt her heart sink. 'I must warn you, I'm rather bored with the neighbourhood crisis. Sylvia goes on and on about it.'

'Sylvia?' Candy stared at her blankly. 'But Sylvia doesn't know anything about it.'

'I'll put the kettle on – ' Kay made a feeble attempt to delay the inevitable confidences.

'Damn the kettle!' Candy said and burst into tears.

'Come in here and sit down.' Kay shepherded her out of the hallway quickly before Emma's sharp ears could become attuned to drama in the atmosphere.

'I can't bear it!' Candy slumped into a chair, groping for a handkerchief. 'I've tried, but – '

After an anxious glance up the stairs, Kay closed the door, hoping that Emma was too absorbed in her books to realize that they had company and come down to join them.

'You're not upset about the new squatter, then?' she probed gently.

'The black man?' Sheer amazement stopped Candy's tears. 'You didn't imagine I cared about *him*? I'm glad he's there. I hope he stays for ever. While he's there, no one else can be!'

'Oh dear!' Kay sat down abruptly, beginning to suspect the real problem.

'You're the only one I can talk to,' Candy said. 'Because it was going on all the time you were away. That means it couldn't be Crispian. You're the only one who's out of it.'

'The shadowy figure – ' Kay did not pretend to misunderstand. 'The vaguely familiar-looking man you saw going in – '

'*Sneaking* in,' Candy corrected. 'I've seen him half a dozen times now. Always when it's dark . . . always late enough so that the kids would be asleep . . .' She hesitated, then took a deep breath and blurted out the final accusation.

'And always when I've been watching for Nick to come home!' Candy closed her eyes and leaned back in her chair, limp with the relief of having been able to tell someone at last.

'I see.' Kay felt limp herself. 'But you can't think it's Nick. That first time you saw him, you were watching for Nick and he came along *after* the other man had gone into the Norris house. Don't you remember?'

'I lied.' Candy opened her eyes and raised her chin defiantly. 'You were all staring at me and I knew what you were thinking. We're the youngest couple in Crozier Crescent and the ones who moved in most recently. None of you knew very much about us or where we came from. Or what kind of crazy friends we might have had – and told about the empty house. I could see that it was more comfortable for you to believe that he was irresponsible and didn't have any morals and he was the only one likely to do a thing like that.'

'It never crossed my mind,' Kay said truthfully.

'Maybe not yours, but I could see Sylvia thinking it. Yes, and Alice, too – it was so much more comforting to think that than to think it might have been her son . . . or her husband.'

'It *did* happen after Norman came home.' It might explain the deterioration in Norman's health. If he were racketing about, trying to carry on a double life under the sharp eyes of his parents and his son, no wonder the nervous strain was beginning to tell.

'Anyway, I lied about Nick,' Candy said flatly. 'He *did* come home that night, but not until much, much later. I was nearly frantic.' She closed her eyes again.

'I still am. Every time he's late beyond a certain hour, I watch out of the window and I see that figure sneaking into the Norris house. I can't stand it much longer!'

'But are you sure it's Nick? Have you seen it clearly enough to identify him?'

'No. He's too clever. It's always so dark and he keeps well into the shadows. Once I even thought – '

'Yes?' Kay encouraged.

'You'll think I'm clutching at straws. Perhaps I am. But once I thought it looked like Mr Norris. Of course, I never saw all that much of him, but I was almost convinced it was him.'

'But surely he'd have let Sylvia know he was coming – '

'Would you?' Candy asked. For a moment they shared the knowledge that there were more comfortable people to have around when a scene was pending. If Mr Norris had flown back abruptly, arriving tired and late at night, he might have preferred to face the intruders without Sylvia at his elbow, however well-intentioned her moral support.

'Anyway,' Candy said, 'it was just that one time. And it couldn't have been. Otherwise, where is he? No – ' she wavered between tears and anger – 'no, I'm afraid it's Nick. I'm terribly afraid it's Nick!'

'I don't believe it,' Kay said. 'Why should Nick want to go prowling over there? You're younger than Elf, and prettier. What could she have to offer – ?'

'She's available,' Candy said bitterly, anger winning. 'Never underestimate the attraction of *that*!'

'Well, what about the nights when Nick is home? Have you seen anyone on those nights?'

'I don't watch out of the windows when Nick is home,' Candy said practically. 'Why should I? When he's with me, I'm not worrying.'

Or perhaps she'd rather not know for certain. So long as she didn't look out of the window while Nick was at home, she could allow herself the hope that perhaps someone else *was* moving through the shadows towards the Norris house. If she looked out and saw no one, then her worst suspicions would be confirmed. The same held true about asking Nick outright.

'Anyway,' Candy sat up, tucked her handkerchief away briskly, and forced a smile. 'It's all right tonight. Crispian is with him, so I can relax.' She spoiled the vote of confidence by the sudden anxiety that shadowed her face.

'Crispian will stay with him . . . won't he?'

'It's all settled.' Crispian sailed in on a gust of euphoria and Scotch. 'We're going over there tomorrow night.'

'Where?' Although Candy had left earlier in order to be home when Nick got back, Kay was still half swamped in the emotional undertow of her wake.

'Sinbad came down to the pub,' Crispian said triumphantly. 'I thought he might. Of course, Elf was with him – '

'She left those children alone?'

'It's all right – Wade stayed with them. I gather he acts as baby-sitter more often than not.'

'What use would he be in an emergency – the state

he's usually in?' Through her indignation, Kay was aware that she sounded like Sylvia. She didn't care. Even Sylvia got her priorities right once in a while.

'Actually,' Crispian admitted, 'it doesn't matter. The eldest child – Poppy – has everything under control. She's a very reliable little thing, they tell me. If anything went wrong, she'd be able to handle it.'

'It isn't fair.' Kay shuddered. Poppy was roughly the same age as Emma. 'It's too much of a burden to put on a child of that age.'

'She doesn't mind.' Crispian yawned and started for the stairs. 'She enjoys it.'

'Who says so?' Kay challenged.

He stopped, puzzled. 'Why, Elf.'

'And you'd believe *her*?' Kay snorted. But that, too, was a Sylvia-type reaction and she was immediately uncomfortable.

'Responsibility doesn't do children any harm at all.' Again, Crispian seemed to be quoting. 'It prepares them for life.'

'I should think that poor child has seen all the life she can handle.'

'You're exaggerating.' He started forward again purposefully, his mind already travelling ahead to some distant point.

Kay followed after him, turning out the lights. 'Did you have a nice evening?' she asked, although conscious that he had not enquired about her evening with Candy. Just as well. Candy's story wouldn't find his ear sympathetic.

'It was . . . fruitful, I think.' He nodded judiciously. 'Yes, I could say it was definitely fruitful.'

'Oh?' Kay got the impression that she was not the only one holding back information. 'Who else was down at the pub? Anyone we know?'

'No one special. A few regulars. Knew them by sight, but couldn't put names to them.' He snapped on the bedroom light and removed his coat and tie. 'Odd, though – '

'What was?'

'I thought – ' He yawned and began unbuttoning his shirt. 'I thought I saw Norman – just a glimpse. In the doorway. He looked in, saw us, and then – just when I thought he was going to come in and join us – he wasn't there any more.'

'That *is* strange.' Kay tried to nudge Crispian towards a conclusion. 'I wonder why he changed his mind when he saw you all?'

'Couldn't have been Norman, after all,' Crispian said. 'Just someone with a vague resemblance. Otherwise, he'd have come over and had a drink with us.'

CHAPTER XI

'Come in!' Sinbad threw the door wide, beaming. 'Come right in!'

As they moved through the hallway, Kay was aware of a pale shadowy form lurking indecisively at the end of the hall. Wade, presumably. She wondered if he were going to join them and what state he would be in.

'You came!' Elf billowed up from the sofa to greet them. She rushed forward joyously, hands outstretched. The newspaper she had been reading fell to the floor, pages fluttering in all directions.

'Yes.' Crispian struggled to free his captured hand, startled by the fulsomeness of this greeting. 'Weren't you expecting us? I thought we'd arranged to last night.'

'I know,' Elf said. 'But lots of people say they'll come, and then they don't, after all.' Her voice was wistful, but resigned. 'Maybe they never meant to. Or maybe they just forget next day.'

'These people came,' Sinbad reminded her. 'So let's ask them to sit down.'

'Oh yes. Of course.' Elf looked around vaguely, seeming faintly surprised to find the room so full of places to sit. She was undoubtedly more accustomed to sitting on floors in derelict houses. 'Sit anywhere – ' She waved an expansive hand. 'Anywhere at all.'

In the background, Poppy quietly gathered up the fallen newspaper, smoothing out the pages, rearranging them in their proper sequence and folding it up neatly. She placed it on a corner of the coffee table – the only clear space on the table – and looked around.

Kay moved hesitantly in the direction of an armchair. Before she reached it, Poppy darted forward and removed a pair of unwashed tights and a couple of cardigans from it. She darted out of the room with them.

'I haven't really had time to get this place into any sort of proper order,' Elf apologized comfortably. 'We haven't been here very long.'

Kay would have liked to have heard Sylvia's reaction to that.

'Now, then.' Sinbad played host. 'Would you like a beer? Or I brought in some duty-free Scotch? Coffee, tea, if you prefer? Even some lemonade – I mean lemon squash.'

'You're American!' Kay suddenly identified the unobtrusive accent. Yet why should she be surprised? According to all the reports, Wade was an American, too.

'That's right.' Sinbad beamed pleasantly at her.

'Beer will be fine,' Crispian said democratically. She noticed that he was unmoved by the revelation. So he had already known. He might have mentioned it.

'I'd like lemon squash.' She realized that Sinbad was still waiting for her reply.

'Coming right up.' He wheeled and left the room.

'Now this is really lovely,' Elf said. 'Just the way it should be. All friends together.' She re-seated herself on the sofa with a contented sigh.

Poppy perched on the arm of the chair Sinbad had been sitting in, and eyed them warily: a sentinel on guard duty, not at all sure of the intentions of the invading strangers. Friends or foes? Kay had the sudden poignant awareness that Poppy was not unaccustomed to neighbourhood delegations and sessions which ended stormily.

She tried to smile reassuringly at Poppy, but was met with a blank stare.

'Here we are.' Sinbad came back into the room carrying a tray. Jasmine trailed behind him with a plate of cheese and crackers, and a proud smile which said that she had been out in the kitchen fixing up the treat all by herself.

'Thank you.' Kay accepted the glass from Sinbad and a cracker overlapped by a jagged wedge of cheese from Jasmine. 'Don't these look delicious? Did you make them all by yourself?'

Jasmine blushed with pleasure and moved on to Crispian, who abstractedly helped himself to four crackers, which was – in its way – just as much of a compliment. Heady with success, Jasmine proffered the plate to her mother.

'You know I'm dieting, darling.' Elf waved Jasmine away. Jasmine retreated to her father's sheltering arm, while Elf gave Kay a conspiratorial look and continued, 'Isn't it awful, the way the pounds roll on when one isn't noticing?'

Apparently, Elf had not been noticing for quite some time. Kay smiled vaguely and allowed her gaze to rove away, hoping the assessing element in it was not too discernible.

At least the wallpaper wasn't hanging off the wall in strips. It passed muster quite well, in fact, except for a few crayoned scrawls at floorboard level. The carpet was another matter. Already it was splatted with stains, blotched with amorphous introdden shapes of discarded or dropped bits of bygone meals.

'I don't believe one ought to be a slave to possessions.' Elf followed Kay's gaze and trotted out the moth-eaten credo as though it were fresh and newly-minted by herself. 'I mean, one shouldn't let *things* matter, should one?'

Especially when they're not your own things. Kay bit back the retort and tried to smile noncommittally. She could feel Crispian's anxious eyes on her. For some obscure reason, it was important to him to keep on good terms with these ghastly people – even if it meant alienating the neighbours and friends they had known for years.

What *was* he up to?

'Where's Emma?' Jasmine rescued her.

'Emma's home in bed. That's why we can't stay too long.' She hoped her tone was neutral enough not to imply disapproval of children still awake and about at this hour.

'That's not a bad idea about bed,' Sinbad said. 'You kids ought to be getting ready for bed, too.'

'No.' Jasmine sprang into his lap as he sat down. 'Not yet. Not yet.'

'It's early,' Elf said. 'I remember how I always hated to go to bed when I was a kid. I don't think kids should be forced to do anything they don't want to do. I think they should be untrammelled spirits.'

'Come on.' Poppy slipped down off the arm of the chair and tugged at Jasmine's skirt. 'Sinbad wants us to go to bed now.'

'Just a little while longer.' Jasmine twined her arms around her father's neck and clung to him. 'Please.'

'Tell you what,' Sinbad compromised. 'You go get into your pyjamas, and then you can come back and sit with us for just a little bitty while.'

Jasmine slid reluctantly from his lap and hurried from the room with Poppy. 'We'll be right back,' she promised. 'Don't say anything until we get back.'

'Kids!' Sinbad shook his head, smiling. 'What can you do with them?'

'You can let them stay up,' Elf said. 'They want to.'

'They're half asleep now,' Sinbad said. 'They'll be dead to the world in half an hour. Just you see.' He straightened and frowned. 'Where's the baby?'

'Heather?' Elf looked around vaguely. 'She was here a minute ago. Maybe she's out with Wade. He'll look after her.'

'He can't even look after himself.' Sinbad got to his feet in a swift catlike movement, then remembered their guests. 'If you'll excuse me a minute, folks.'

'Just carry on as usual,' Crispian waved careless

permission. 'Don't let us interfere with your routine.'

'It isn't exactly a routine – ' Sinbad was halfway between wry amusement and annoyance.

'She'll turn up,' Elf said serenely. 'She always does.'

'Well, just for the novelty of it – ' Sinbad turned his annoyance on Elf, with some justification – 'why don't you start looking for her?'

Elf shrugged and left the room languidly. Sinbad looked after her for a moment, then smiled as Poppy and Jasmine rushed in, having broken all records at getting into their pyjamas.

'You kids seen the baby anywhere?' he asked.

'She was on the floor in the corner.' Trust Poppy to have been keeping an eye on things. 'She was asleep, but she kept waking up and crawling around a bit and then going back to sleep again – '

Jasmine helpfully looked under one of the chairs, but Poppy crossed to the sofa and looked behind it. 'Here she is,' she announced, pulling the baby out into their view.

Not surprisingly, the baby began to cry at this sudden and rude intrusion into her dreams.

'All right, Heather.' Sinbad swept her up into his arms and cradled her against him. 'Don't get noisy. It's all right. You should be in your own little bed, not sleeping behind the furniture. Don't you know that?'

'I was going to put her to bed.' Poppy was instantly on the defensive. 'I meant to. Only I was trying to clean this place before the people came and I forgot.'

'I wasn't blaming *you*.' Sinbad's face darkened. 'You do your best, Lord knows.' He turned his head to the doorway, but there was no sign of Elf. Was she looking for Heather, or had she settled down comfortably in the kitchen to chat with Wade until the crisis had blown over?

'Come on.' Sinbad started for the door. 'Let's get all you kids to bed.'

'No! No!' Jasmine hurled herself into his path.

'Please, Sinbad – ' Poppy caught at his elbow.

'Don't let us disturb your routine,' Crispian said again. 'You go ahead and do what you usually do when you're putting them to bed . . .' He hesitated just a fraction too long and it came out a shade too eagerly. 'Sing to them . . . or whatever.'

'No!' Poppy, too, had caught the change in his tone and instinctively mistrusted it. 'Don't sing tonight, Sinbad. Instead, tell us – Please, tell us again – '

'Tell you what we goin' to do? Someday? Someday . . .' Sinbad looked down at them and sighed. Their faces turned up to him expectantly.

'Tell us,' Jasmine echoed. 'Please tell us – '

'Okay,' he sighed again. 'But then you gotta go to bed. And no more arguments.'

'We promise, Sinbad,' Poppy said for all of them.

'Well, someday . . .' He settled himself in the armchair again, the baby in his lap. Jasmine pushed Heather to one side so that she could also fit on to his lap. Poppy resumed her perch on the arm of his chair. They waited, in a breathless captivated expectancy.

After one slightly awkward and self-conscious glance across at Kay and Crispian, he appeared to forget their presence. He looked down at the children again, the only audience he cared about.

'Someday,' he said softly, 'after a few more voyages, I'll have enough money saved to buy us a boat of our own. A nice big boat, big enough for all of us, and we'll leave the land and all its hassles behind – and we'll go sailing. There's a great big beautiful world out there, and we'll sail ourselves right across it, and up it, and down it, and we'll see us it all. All the big beautiful harbours, all the funny frowsty little ports. We'll drop anchor in them all, and when we're tired of them and we've seen all they've got to show us, then we'll sail out again and head off into the horizon to find new places.'

You see – ? Poppy shot a drowsy triumphant look at Kay and Crispian. *We won't always be here in your way.* She slid lower on her perch to rest her head on Sinbad's broad shoulder. 'Tell us about the islands,' she murmured.

'Oh yes, the islands.' Sinbad dropped into a lulling sing-song chant. 'All those beautiful islands. Even their names are beautiful. We'll sail to all of them. To the Spice Islands and the Windward Islands, the Orkney Islands and the Shetland Islands, the Virgin Islands and the Canary Islands, the Philippine Islands and the Galapagos Islands – '

Heather had gone back to sleep, Jasmine's eyelids were drooping. Poppy snuggled her head closer to Sinbad's.

'To the West Indies and the East Indies . . .' He lowered his voice still more, it was almost a lullaby. 'We'll see us Easter Island and Sable Island and Pitcairn Island and Hispaniola . . .'

Jasmine was asleep. Gently, not disturbing either sleeping child, Sinbad waggled his shoulder to lift Poppy's head and slid forward in his chair.

'We'll visit us the Mariana Islands and the Solomon Islands . . .' Without breaking the rhythm, he rose to his feet carrying the children. 'And Tonga and Sarawak, and the Sandwich Islands . . .'

His voice faded as he stepped into the hallway and began to climb the stairs. Poppy trailed after him, half-asleep, half-mesmerized.

'The Pied Piper!' Kay exclaimed softly, half under the spell herself.

'Yes.' Crispian settled back in his chair, looking oddly smug. 'Yes, I rather think he is.'

CHAPTER XII

'How nice of you to find the time to come over this evening.' Sylvia looked at Kay and Crispian coldly. 'We were afraid you might be too busy with your new-found friends, weren't we, Jeremy?'

'Hmm?' Jeremy did not appear to be afraid of anything except running out of drink. He was taking painstaking inventory at the bar. 'That's right,' he agreed absently. 'Long time no see.'

'We saw you visiting those people the other night,' Sylvia underlined, in case they had missed her displeasure. 'I hope you had a nice time.'

'It was very fruitful,' Crispian said. It was the only comment he had made to Kay about the evening, as well.

'It seems to have given Crispian a lot to think about,' Kay goaded, although it was unlikely that he would be more forthcoming with Sylvia and Jeremy than he had been with her.

'I'm not surprised.' Sylvia twitched an eyebrow and waited. It was a technique which usually elicited an apology from Jeremy, but Kay was not dependent upon her approval and Crispian didn't even notice.

'Jeremy, come and sit down!' Sylvia seemed to become aware of her husband's curious reluctance to become part of the group.

'Er, yes, quite. Just let me top everyone up.' Jeremy made a quick swoop with the appropriate bottles before alighting in the most distant chair, managing to edge it farther away.

'I *do* think you ought to show more discretion,' Sylvia said. 'It's bad enough to have Marjorie popping in and out of that place all the time.'

'Oh, well,' Crispian said comfortably. 'They're here now and I think Marjorie is right. We might as well learn to live with them.'

There was a muffled sound as Jeremy pushed his chair yet farther back. Not content with merely fence-sitting, he was now trying to re-align the fence.

'That's all very well for you, Crispian,' Sylvia said tartly. 'But you're not here living with them all day. Haven't you seen what it's like when they all swarm out into the yard and lie around?'

'It's summer,' Crispian said. 'It's only natural – '

'Are you suggesting – ?' Sylvia asked dangerously. 'Seriously suggesting that it will be better in the winter when they have to stay indoors? What will they do to the house?' She turned to Kay, not waiting for his answer. 'What have they done to the house already?'

'It's not so bad.' Kay felt she was being a disappointment by not reporting wholesale depredation. 'The Norrises will have to send the carpets away to be cleaned – or perhaps get new ones. And, of course, re-paper.'

'Aha!' Sylvia had suspected as much. 'Those children can't be expected to know how to behave in a proper home. I don't suppose they're even housebroken!'

'Oh, I say!' Jeremy stirred uncomfortably.

'I didn't mean it that way.' Sylvia took him up sharply. 'Although I'd have my doubts about the youngest. But the best of children are unmanageable at times and have no respect for property unless they've been taught properly. How could a woman like that teach them anything?'

'I don't know why you're so harsh on her.' Jeremy's chair gained a bit more distance.

'And I don't know what you should care. She isn't one of your AB consumption-oriented class. Try her out on one of your surveys, if you don't believe me. She'd probably come up on your rating as minus YZ.'

'There's no such category.' For a moment, Jeremy was on firm ground.

'You'd have to make one for her.' The sands shifted under him again. 'How else could you categorize someone who moves into another woman's house, accompanied by a man who is certainly in no condition to support her, and lives off the State with her three little bastards.'

'Oh, I say!' Jeremy winced away again. If his chair slid any farther back, he would be up against the wall. 'That's coming it a bit strong.'

'Is it?' Sylvia was grim. 'And now she's got a second man over there. At least he seems to have a bit of money. Does *that* put her into one of your acceptable consumer categories?'

'Sinbad is just visiting them,' Kay put in hastily, trying to draw some of the fire from Jeremy out of mercy. 'He works on a ship and he'll be reporting back for duty when his leave is over.'

'We've heard *that* one before,' Sylvia sneered. 'And Norman is still around.'

'I wouldn't think there's much comparison,' Crispian said. 'Sinbad is perfectly healthy. Not a nerve in his body – anyway, not that kind.'

'Quite the little international conclave here in Crozier Crescent, aren't we?' Jeremy seemed taken with the idea. 'Norman, from an airline; Sinbad, from a shipping line; and the Norrises, who are always flying or sailing somewhere exotic.'

'That's right!' It was obviously an aspect of the situation that Sylvia hadn't considered before. 'It makes you wonder if they might have met, doesn't it?'

'Oh, I don't know,' Jeremy said. 'The world's a big place.'

'Not these days. As you've just pointed out. I'll bet they have.' Sylvia rushed on to make the connection more quickly than any of them could – or were willing to –

follow. 'If the Norrises were on that black man's ship and he found out their address and knew that they were going to be out of England for any length of time, then he could have told his . . . his paramour . . . that the coast was clear for her to take over their house.'

There was a thud as Jeremy's chair hit the wall.

'Not necessarily.' Crispian considered the idea. 'Why couldn't it have been Norman? It's much more likely that the Norrises would have been on one of his flights – they'd have arranged it especially, no doubt. You know how they love those little personal bits in their travelogues about being invited up to the flight deck to visit the pilot and all that. They'd get a lot more personal attention with Norman piloting. In fact, I seem to recall his mentioning that they've done it a couple of times. Fortunately, they don't fly everywhere, or I think he'd find them a bit of a nuisance. But, when you think of it, that's the more logical explanation. They'd talk to him about their future plans and the length of time they expected to be out of the country in a way they'd never confide in a stranger. So, why couldn't it have been Norman who passed the information on?'

'Because his own family live practically across the street.' Sylvia exonerated Norman triumphantly. 'He wouldn't want to let people like that move in so close. He knows it would ruin property values in the neighbourhood.'

'Ah – ' Crispian was now happily lost in the intellectual exercise. It had no reality for him at all, Kay saw. Whereas Sylvia was in deadly earnest. 'But he might have a reason that would outweigh that consideration. Suppose he were blackmailed into it?'

'Why should Norman be blackmailed?'

'He's been flying some very strange routes – especially in the early days.' Crispian was improvising merrily, unaware that any of his listeners might be taking him seriously. 'Suppose he got mixed up in drugs at some point? Perhaps smuggling them in to London and supplying them to hippies? To Wade – who recognized him when he ran across him again recently and threatened to shop him to the police unless – '

'Jeremy!' Sylvia interrupted crossly. 'What *are* you doing?'

Trying to crawl up the wall, from the look of it. Having edged his chair away as far as it would go, Jeremy now seemed to be attempting to swing it around at an angle that would leave him with his back to the room. One could understand that he wished to dissociate himself from what was becoming an obsession on Sylvia's part, but surely this was going too far.

'Oh, er, rug got rucked up around the chair leg. I was just trying to fix it.'

'Well, it wouldn't if you'd stop fidgeting around. I don't see why you can't sit still for a minute. You must have built up an immunity to those tranquillizers – it's time you switched to some different ones.'

'Oh yes. Quite right. Good idea. Hadn't thought of that.' Jeremy lurched out of his chair and headed for the bar. 'Another drink? We can all use another one.'

Sylvia watched him with a worried frown. Even Crispian had lost the thread of his argument as Jeremy clattered bottles and glasses, perilously close to dropping them.

'Perhaps,' Crispian said thoughtfully, 'it might be wise to stop the tranquillizers altogether for a bit. They may be having side effects you aren't aware of yet.'

'That could be an even better idea,' Sylvia said. 'One drug addict in the neighbourhood is enough.'

'Now that's too much!' Jeremy seemed to realize that he had bared his teeth like a cornered animal and hastily twitched his lips, transforming the snarl into an inadequate smile. 'I mean to say, the account is a quarter of a million pounds billing. And the clients are very proud of the fact that their Agency people actually use the product. It could ruin everything if I stopped taking them.'

'It could ruin you if you don't,' Sylvia said. 'Do you think Rupert and I want you sitting around the house like that . . . that *creature* across the street?' Sylvia looked as though she could do with a couple of tranquillizers herself.

'That's nonsense!' Jeremy was showing rare signs of fight, the danger of being separated from his pills provoking a reaction that the prospect of plummeting property values had never touched off.

It's time to go . . . Let's get out of here . . . The two messages crossed as Kay and Crispian met each other's eyes. Crispian moved forward in his chair.

'Here you are, old man.' A drink was thrust into his hand, forcing him back again. 'Sorry about that. Sylvia's a bit on edge these days.' Jeremy pushed another drink at Kay with desperate pleading in his eyes. 'We both are.'

They settled back in their chairs, trapped for the length of time it would take them to finish the drinks.

'That's better.' Jeremy leaned against the wall, in a position to intercept anyone who tried to leave. 'How's the music business these days?'

'Business? Music?' As an attempt to change the subject, it left something to be desired. Crispian's response, for instance. 'Very dull.' He looked at Jeremy suspiciously. 'Why?'

'*Why?*' Jeremy shook his head groggily. 'No reason. No reason at all, old man. Just trying to make civilized conversation. You know, be sociable. I'll admit it's getting to be a forgotten art around here these days, but you don't need to get uptight about it.'

'I'm not uptight.' Perhaps not, but he was on guard. Crispian relaxed with an almost visible effort. 'You just lost me for a minute there, that's all.'

'If you ask me – ' Sylvia had been brooding over the

original subject – 'that child is a drug addict, too.'

Jeremy leaped, spilling his drink. 'What child?' He mopped at his shirt front in exasperation. 'What are you on about now?'

'The youngest one. You can see it's his.'

'I don't know how you can be so certain about that,' Jeremy said. 'I'd always understood an addict that far gone wasn't able – I mean, they're uninterested and, er, incapable.'

'The child is getting on for two years old,' Sylvia calculated swiftly. 'Add another nine months on to that. He wouldn't have been so far gone that long ago.'

'Hmm.' Jeremy seemed to be doing some calculations of his own. 'I suppose you could be right.'

'Of course I'm right,' Sylvia said. 'You just have to look at that child. Bloodless, boneless and brainless – it's the image of him.'

'It is, you know.' Kay was more readily convinced than Jeremy. She recalled her first sight of Wade and Heather together, propped up against the front steps, impassive and immobile, both gazing out at the world with the same vacant, incurious stare.

'*And* it's a well-known fact,' Sylvia went on. 'Babies can be drug addicts when they're born – with parentage like that.'

'I think that's just when the mother is a drug addict herself,' Kay said. 'The baby gets it through the bloodstream. I don't think the father's being one can have any effect on it.'

'The mother probably is,' Sylvia sniffed. 'Just look at the way she goes around. You can't call her a normal woman.'

'No, but I don't think she's an addict, either.' Kay frowned, considering the idea. Elf was lost to the world certainly, but not in any drug-induced way. Rather, she had chosen to live on a different plane and did not need artificial stimulus to keep her on her selected high. It was a choice a lot of Elf's generation had made in their teenage years, but most of them had found their way back into society's fold by now. Elf was one of those who stubbornly persisted in being the embodiment of the Spirit of the 'Sixties, not noticing that the chill wind of the 'Seventies had blown most of their illusions away.

'Well, you'll never convince me of that,' Sylvia said. 'And you can't deny she's a bad influence to have around.'

'More sad than bad, I'd say.' Elf's lifestyle was not likely to inspire any local followers. With gratitude, Kay recalled Emma's distaste for Wade. Nor were Rupert and Barnaby in any danger of being seduced by that way of life, even if it did have the plus of not enforcing baths. There was something to be said for the natural healthy snobbishness of children.

'That's your opinion,' Sylvia snapped. 'I don't happen to share it. And when the Norrises get back – '

Crispian leaped to his feet and started forward. Too late. Once again, Jeremy, his frame ravaged by tranquillizers and alcohol, pitched face forward to the floor.

CHAPTER XIII

'It's gone beyond a joke,' Kay said, as soon as Emma had left the breakfast table in the morning. 'Someone ought to do something.'

'What do you suggest we do?' Crispian asked reasonably. 'You heard me warn him. I can't take his pills away and hide them. That's for Sylvia to do – if she gets worried enough.'

'Even then, he'd just get more. I gather there are bottles of them floating all around the agency, for photography and label design and all that sort of thing. Sylvia says he doesn't even have a prescription for them. He just brings more home when he's run out.'

'There you are.' Crispian shrugged. 'It's up to him, then.'

'But they can't be safe. Just look at what they're doing to him.'

'What do you suggest?' Crispian asked again. 'An anonymous letter to the manufacturer telling him that his product is dangerous and possibly unfit for human consumption? That would go down well. Especially if Jeremy ever discovered we were responsible for it.'

'You know I don't mean that.' Kay glanced out of the window and stiffened. Emma, with elaborate unconcern, was drifting across the street, a book under her arm. Poppy was in the front yard, watching her approach.

'In any case,' Crispian said. 'The things are probably perfectly safe. They have to pass all sorts of tests. Of course, you're usually warned not to mix them with alcohol. As always, the use or abuse is up to the ultimate consumer. To Jeremy. But I must admit, he does seem to be making a balls-up of it.'

'He's cracking up. I wonder – ' Kay voiced the thought which had occurred to her during the night. 'Do you suppose he's passing them around? Sharing them with Norman? Norman seems to be in nearly as bad a state, although I don't think he drinks to the extent that Jeremy does.'

'Jeremy has been knocking it back of late,' Crispian agreed. He considered the new idea. 'It's possible, I suppose, but I doubt it. Norman was in pretty bad shape when he first showed up. I don't think you can blame medication for that. I think the medical check-up caught him at that point just before he started to go down, where he had to go down before he started coming up again.'

'He hasn't started up yet, that I can see,' Kay said. She hesitated. 'Did you believe what you were saying last night? About the drugs? Do you think Norman might have passed from smuggling them to taking them himself?'

'Not really. It would have been caught in the routine medical long before this. He was probably pushing himself to the limits of his endurance, worrying about Barnaby and his parents and whether to send him to boarding school, and the fees – ' He paused and studied Kay with interest.

She was staring at something happening outside, her hands making abortive little grabbing motions, as though to snatch something back.

'You're getting pretty jumpy yourself,' he observed cheerfully. 'What's the matter? Don't tell me it's a neighbourhood epidemic?'

'Why shouldn't it be?' Kay turned on him, suddenly snappish. 'I can understand why Sylvia gets upset. Those people are disrupting the atmosphere in a way she never dreamed of. We never had suspicions like these about each other before the squatters moved in. No wonder everyone is a nervous wreck.'

'I don't see why it should bother everyone,' Crispian said. 'The only people directly concerned are the Norrises – and they aren't worrying about it.'

'The Norrises don't know about it yet.'

'There you are. "What the eye does not see" – ' He broke off, noticing that his levity was unappreciated.

'What's so fascinating out there?'

'Emma. She's gone over to play with those children. I *asked* her to stay in the house.'

'The children are there.' Crispian pushed back his chair. 'It's unreasonable to expect her to keep away from them.'

'Especially since we've visited over there.' Kay knew, but still had mixed feelings about it. Of course, she would not allow herself to be swayed by Sylvia's obvious and much-voiced disapproval; yet, at the same time, she found Crispian's attitude nearly as disconcerting. In some obscure way, he seemed almost to be urging Emma forward into a closer liaison with the squatter children. Or was that just her imagination?

'By the way – ' Crispian was at the window – 'isn't it time to give Emma her pocket money?'

'Not until tomorrow.'

'Oh, well.' He was nodding with inward satisfaction at something he saw. 'It doesn't do to be too rigid about rules. Not during the holidays. Why don't I nip over and give it to her now?'

'Because it will establish a precedent, ruin discipline, and – '

But the door had slammed shut on her answer. He had never had any intention of heeding it.

Kay went over to the window, pulled back the curtain and stood watching the scene with no attempt at concealment.

Beaming broadly, Crispian counted out change into

the hand of a surprised but delighted Emma. As though he had not noticed their presence before, he discovered Poppy and Jasmine watching intently. He beamed upon them, reached into his pocket again and distributed impartial largesse.

Get yourself an ice-cream. Kay did not need to hear the words. She had seen the same expression on his face so many times when he had said the same thing to Emma.

Sinbad came out of the house. He exchanged a few words with the children before glancing at Crispian. Then he, too, put his hand in his pocket. He gave money to his bemused brood, and then bestowed a coin upon Emma. Going Crispian one better, he patted Emma on the head.

Not so bemused by their good fortune that they were willing to allow the adults time for second thoughts, the children danced off down the street in the direction of the shops, yelping with joy.

Crispian and Sinbad watched their departure with fond smiles, then turned back to each other and settled down to conversation.

Kay snapped the curtains shut as violently as possible, despite the knowledge that it was an empty gesture. No one was watching.

Kay was in the kitchen when Crispian eventually returned. Hearing the front door close, she began to register disapproval by slamming a few dishes about.

'Ah, there you are.' Careless of the storm signals blowing, Crispian sailed into the kitchen. One of his ports of call had obviously been the pub.

'We're going to a barbecue tonight.' He imparted the news as though he expected her to cheer.

'Who?'

'You, me, Emma . . .' He looked around. 'That's all

there are of us. Just us three.'

'Oh? And who's giving the barbecue?' Not that she had any doubt.

'Sinbad. He's bought a barbecue for the kids and is breaking it in tonight. Very American – a back-yard barbecue with good old hamburgers. They'd die of starvation, you know, if they couldn't get their hamburgers. They'd just curl up and pine away.'

'I suppose you told them we'd go.'

'Of course I told them we'd go. Haven't I just said so?' Crispian regained control quickly and, obviously intent on placating her, offered, 'Marjorie is coming, too.'

'Marjorie is not the social arbiter of this community!'

'Neither is Sylvia!'

They glared at each other briefly and Crispian was the first to turn his eyes away.

'We're going,' he said flatly. 'It's very important to me that we do. It's important to all of us.'

'What – ?'

But he had already divulged more than he had intended. He left the room abruptly. She heard the front door slam and knew that it would be some time before she saw him again.

CHAPTER XIV

The new portable barbecue might have been bought by Sinbad, but the sun lounges, the chairs, the cushions, the dishes, the cutlery, all belonged to the Norrises. Kay realized this in her first swift glance around and then tried to put it out of her mind.

Certainly, it didn't bother Marjorie. She was reclining in one of the sun lounges, glass in hand, watching as Sinbad assembled the barbecue and tried to organize his willing but inexpert helpers. She was probably taking mental notes.

Poppy was earnestly splitting the round flat buns; Jasmine was spooning sweet pickle into a small bowl; Heather, showing unusual animation, was stuffing her mouth with potato crisps. They were, Kay saw thankfully, from a small packet which was obviously hers: an extra-large bag was still unopened. Even Wade looked halfway alive as he struggled to undo a sack of charcoal.

Elf, stretched out on the other sun lounge, raised a languid hand in greeting. 'Sit down,' she said. 'Emma, help yourself to a Coke. Sinbad, drinks for Kay and Crispian!'

'Comin' right up.' Totally unself-conscious in a shiny apron proclaiming CHIEF COOK AND BOTTLE WASHER, Sinbad uncapped two bottles, poured the contents of one into a glass for Kay and handed the other bottle to Crispian.

Cushions had been plumped up invitingly on the white-painted wrought-iron chairs which had also, Kay noted, been freshly washed. At least it appeared that the Norrises' belongings were being cared for – while Sinbad was around.

But she could not settle back easily, as Marjorie had done. She was too conscious of the fact that, by being here with them, she was appearing to give a seal of respectability to the activities of the interlopers. She glanced uneasily at Crispian, but found no comfort there.

'Well, cheers!' Crispian tilted the bottle and drank as though he had never known what it was to use a glass. Watching him, Emma lifted her tin of Coke and did the same. There went discipline.

'Oh, it's a party.' Sinbad had caught her wince.

'They're only young once,' Elf said indulgently, offering her usual excuse to criticism sensed but not actually noticed.

Poppy looked about surreptitiously, pinpointing the reason for discord. Her own opened tin was on the table by her elbow. Thoughtfully, she prepared another bun before taking a glass and pouring her drink into it. Then, to her sister's amazement, she removed the tin from Jasmine's hand and poured it into another glass.

Marjorie smiled and gave a little registering nod. Kay wondered whether Poppy's gesture would ultimately be recorded under the heading 'Pressure of Peer Group' or 'Social Climbing'.

'Oh, Poppy,' Elf protested. 'Now you've gone and dirtied more glasses.'

'I'll wash them,' Poppy said. 'I do anyway.'

Sinbad's lips tightened. He turned away abruptly and went over to Wade. 'How you coming along, old buddy?' He took the sack of charcoal from Wade's ineffective hands and opened it effortlessly.

'Thanks.' Wade dropped on to the freshly-turned earth of the flower-bed bordering the back-yard and resumed his usual cross-legged slump, breathing heavily from his exertions.

Sinbad poured charcoal into the barbecue, lit it, and put the grill on top.

'Like old times,' Wade said faintly. It was the first time Kay had ever heard him volunteer a comment. He was watching the charcoal smoulder and, for once, really seemed to be seeing what he was looking at.

'Not quite, old buddy,' Sinbad said softly. 'Not quite. But near to it as we're ever goin' to get, these days.'

Wade nodded, then lifted his head and looked above and beyond them, staring at something so intently that Kay turned to follow his gaze.

She saw the wistful blur of Rupert's face in an upstairs window, just before Sylvia appeared behind him and pulled him back. The window slammed down with an explosive sound.

But that hadn't been what Wade was watching; his eyes were really turned inward to contemplate some private vista of his own. The road not taken? The might-have-been? Or was she simply romanticizing? It was more likely that he was merely calculating the length of time until his next fix.

'You kids watch the fire,' Sinbad ordered. 'Make sure it doesn't go out. I'm going in to wash my hands and get the hamburgers out of the fridge. Then we'll start cooking.'

She should be pleased that Sinbad was trying to instil the rudiments of hygiene in the children by his example. Instead, Kay found herself strangely disturbed. It was the casual way he was treating the Norris house as though it were his own. But if the squatters had taken over the house, surely they weren't going to stop short of utilizing all the facilities in it. It was just that it was somehow more noticeable today.

And surely – she tried to remember newspaper stories about other squatters – other squatters weren't so *blatant* about it. Other squatters crouched inside their occupied houses, always leaving someone to guard the place when they went outside, ever-conscious that the rightful owners might return and effect entrance as they themselves had, and that they might find themselves locked out in their turn.

These people acted as though they had reason to know that they need never fear that. As though they knew they had nothing to fear from the Norrises . . . As though they knew the Norrises would never come back.

The earth of the flower-beds was disturbed. It had been newly dug-over.

Kay shook her head as though to shake the thought out of her mind, but it refused to be dislodged. She realized that the seed had been planted there some time ago and had taken root, flowering now like some monstrous flesh-eating jungle plant to disrupt the gentle peace of a suburban English garden.

What if Candy had been right?

What if that figure she had seen – just once – *had* been Mr Norris? Elspeth Norris could have been walking just ahead of him and been out of sight before Candy reached the window.

It was a frighteningly possible explanation of why Sylvia had never received an answering letter from them.

If Sylvia's original letter had reached the Norrises . . .

If they had reacted with the righteous indignation she had expected . . .

If they had cancelled all other plans and immediately boarded the first outgoing flight to London . . . arriving at some unearthly hour of the morning . . . not having bothered to let anyone know that they were on their way because they would be there in person so soon . . .

If they had walked into their house to confront the squatters . . .

'*It couldn't have been*,' Candy had said. '*Otherwise, where is he?*'

Where were they?

Kay looked at Elf, lying back in the lap of a luxury she had probably never known before. To what lengths would she go to hold on to it? At Wade, gazing with an inhuman blankness into space. Could his impassiveness erupt suddenly into murderous fury? Or could he be manipulated by a subtler, more unscrupulous mentality, into an act of violence – which, perhaps, in his drug-dazed state, he would not even be aware of committing?

These people had obviously fallen into the cushiest berth they had ever seen. Would they stop at anything to keep it from being snatched out from under them?

'Here we are.' Sinbad marched through the kitchen door proudly bearing aloft a tray of ready-formed hamburger patties.

He brought with him such a wave of normalcy and geniality that Kay instantly felt ashamed of the wild notions that had been crowding into her brain.

And yet... Of them all, Sinbad was the only one who could have carried through the details of such an operation to a satisfactory – for them – conclusion.

She could visualize Elf, all too clearly, striking a deadly blow. But then the picture dissolved, with Elf leaving the dead bodies on the floor like just another pile of unswept dust. Likewise Wade, having been roused to action, would surely have expended all that remained of his febrile energy in the act itself, leaving nothing for the follow-through necessary to conceal the crime.

But Sinbad was a different matter, made of sterner stuff. Not that she believed him capable of murder – there was something essentially too good-natured about him for that. But, murder having been committed, he would bend his energies to the concealment of it with no more sense of guilt than he ... than he inhabited the house the others had stolen into.

It was not hard to visualize him arriving unsuspecting at Elf's new address and walking in to find his incompetent love and 'old buddy Wade' at a loose end, trying to ignore the fact of a couple of corpses stretched out in the guestroom, hoping like Mr Micawber that something would turn up.

And poor Sinbad had turned up, walking into nightmare, with the choice of turning the mother of his child and his old friend over to the police, or of becoming an accessory after the fact and helping them to conceal the crime.

And so had begun the Good Neighbour Campaign. The tidying up of the Norris property: the pruning of the rose-bushes, the mowing of the grass, the digging over of the flower-beds.

Kay became aware that Crispian was looking at her curiously. Would he believe her if she told him her theory?

Not for a minute. Nor would Marjorie, watching so complacently as her tame squatters, her raw material for some new thesis, went through their innocent-appearing paces. She would not want to believe anything against them.

Sylvia would believe it. But Sylvia would believe anything bad about them.

Was Sylvia's paranoia infecting her?

Kay forced a smile, which Crispian returned dubiously. He apparently did not find it reassuring. But, equally apparently, his mind was elsewhere.

There were sizzling noises and savoury aromas from the barbecue as Sinbad lovingly arranged the hamburger patties on the grill over the glowing coals.

The children gathered round, enchanted. 'Now, Sinbad?' Poppy stood poised with her plate of buns.

'Not quite yet. Just you hold on a minute.' He raised his head and called out. 'All right – who wants theirs rare? Who wants medium? Who wants well-done? Sing out your orders!'

'I'll take mee-dee-ummmm rare.' To Kay's consternation and Emma's embarrassed horror, Crispian did just that, in a sort of modified Gregorian chant. 'If you-ou-ou please . . .'

'Hey, great, man!' Sinbad chortled with appreciation and took up the beat. 'One mee-dee-ee-uu-uum ra-are.'

'And. my. wife. will. too.' Crispian switched to the Habanera.

'And. one. for. Kay.' Sinbad followed him effortlessly.

Emma relaxed, beginning to sense that the ground rules had changed and this occasion was not the same as tea with Rupert under Sylvia's critical eye.

'Well, well, very well done for me.' Elf attempted to take up the refrain, but didn't quite make it.

'Well. done. for. you.' Sinbad nodded at her approvingly, giving her credit for the attempt.

'I'm out of my depth if you're all bursting into song,' Marjorie said. 'But I *would* like mine well done.'

'Then that's the way you'll get it.' It broke the spell and Sinbad reverted to unsung speech. 'Okay, Poppy, quick now, two at a time. Those buns get just the fastest toasting ever – just show 'em to the coals, or they'll burn. Jasmine, you stand by to spread the butter on 'em quick.'

Intent on their tasks, the two elder children hovered over the grill, dividing their anxious attention between the toasting buns and Sinbad, awaiting his further instructions.

'That's it – ' Sinbad lifted the buns with his cooking tongs and put them on the plate. Jasmine pounced to butter them. 'All right, Poppy. Two more now.'

It was all so domestic, so friendly, so *normal*. How could she entertain such suspicions about such lovely people who were in the process of entertaining her so well? How could she suspect such dark deeds, look for sinister undercurrents?

And yet, Crispian had just flown into a towering rage. Kay knew it as surely as she had ever known anything in her life. Without moving a muscle, without disturbing the set smile on his face, he was seething with suppressed fury.

Why?

Everything had been perfectly straightforward and innocent, so far. There had been no possible reason for him to be upset.

But he was.

No one else seemed aware of it. Kay looked around casually. Nothing seemed to have changed.

Elf beamed impartially at everyone, totally relaxed on her – on Elspeth Norris's – sun lounge, untroubled by any sense of wrongdoing or impropriety. Elf's smile widened as Jasmine approached, carefully balancing a plate with a well-done hamburger buried under a tilting pile of crisps, accepting it as her right – the tribute due to the matriarch of the clan.

Heather crouched within Wade's encircling arm beside the rich crumpled earth of the flower-bed, both of them watching the group around the barbecue with just a trace more animation than was usual. Their resemblance was subtle but, now that it had been pointed out, unmistakable. Heredity? Environment? Or were the two inseparable in this case?

Perhaps one ought to ask Marjorie. She was the nearest they had to an expert on the subject.

Turning to observe Marjorie, Kay intercepted Crispian's sudden murderous glare. There was no doubt that, for the moment, at least, he was dangerously close to hating Marjorie.

But why? What had Marjorie done?

'Thank you, dear.' Numbly, she accepted her plate from Jasmine. 'How delicious.'

At the same instant, Marjorie was accepting a plate from Poppy, but with a faintly abstracted air, her smile fading to a puzzled frown, as though she sensed animosity in the air.

'Here we are.' Sinbad carried the plate over to Wade himself. 'Doesn't that look good?'

Heather snatched eagerly for her hamburger and took a big bite, catsup dribbling from the corners of her mouth, but Wade turned his head away.

'Not hungry,' he said. 'I gotta Coke. I'm fine.'

'You want more than a Coke, man.' Sinbad crouched beside him, coaxing. 'Just take a bite and see how good it is. If I do say so myself.'

'Naw . . .' But it was more trouble to resist than to comply. Wade's hands automatically grasped the plate thrust into them.

'That's it,' Sinbad encouraged. 'You know you said it looked like old times, now you tell me if it tastes like old times, too. I didn't buy any old cat's meat they sell for hamburger here, you know, I had this ground special for us.'

So that was why it had so much more flavour, Kay thought, it wasn't just the charcoal grilling. She watched Wade nibble at his hamburger.

'Yeah, it's great, man,' he agreed.

'You don't think there's too much pepper and stuff on it?' Sinbad honestly seemed to be seeking the opinion.

'Naw, just great.' Hardly noticing that he had done so, Wade took another bite. Then, the movement of eating having been established, he continued absently.

Sinbad was doing a wonderful job. Kay realized that Wade already looked healthier than he had a few days ago. A few more ounces of flesh had been added and the beginnings of a faint tan seemed to indicate that he was taking faltering footsteps towards rejoining the human race. She wondered if Sinbad had managed to cut down his drug dosage.

'Good, good.' Sinbad rose to his feet. 'And just wait and see what we've got for dessert. You won't be able to resist *that*.'

CHAPTER XV

As the evening neared its end, the atmosphere was relaxed and companionable. Crispian had even forgiven Marjorie her mysterious transgression. Largely, Kay feared, because Marjorie had announced that she had some work to do and had taken her departure. Crispian's approval had followed her retreat.

The children, drenched in bliss and butter, were popping corn over the glowing charcoal, the final delight of the barbecue. Heather was asleep against Wade's knee. Wade was still cross-legged on the grass, but the other adults were in chairs, Sinbad's close by the grill so that he could keep a protective eye on Poppy, Jasmine and Emma.

'That's enough now – ' He caught Poppy's arm as she was about to tip more kernels into the pan. 'We've got more than we can eat now, and it's no good cold. Save some for another day.'

'No-o-o.' But Jasmine's protest was an automatic reflex, ending in a yawn.

'Yes.' Sinbad laughed again. 'You're almost asleep now. Look at Heather – she's asleep already. Time to call it a day.'

'And Emma's nearly asleep, as well.' Crispian suddenly reached out and captured his startled daughter, pulling her into his lap. 'I'll have to carry her home.'

'All right.' Emma considered the idea and found it not without merit. 'Carry me.' She made herself comfortable.

'No rush,' Sinbad said lazily. 'Have one more for the road.'

'Why not? I'm not driving.'

In the faint light from the barbecue, Kay saw the

sudden glint of Crispian's eyes as he arranged Emma more comfortably. She was unsurprised when he tilted his head back and began to sing softly.

'*Sleep, my child, and peace attend thee,*
'*All through the night* . . .'

It was an open invitation Sinbad could no more refuse than other men could refuse a drink. He swept his own daughter into his arms and took up the refrain.

'*Guardian angels God will send thee,*
'*All through the night* . . .'

Elf waved her hand lazily in rhythm, Wade swayed without dislodging the baby propped against his knee. Kay leaned back in her chair, abruptly aware that this was what Crispian had been angling for all evening.

It was, furthermore, the reason why Crispian had been so furious with Marjorie earlier on. He had just started Sinbad singing when Marjorie had broken the mood and stopped him. But Marjorie had gone home now.

And the songfest was on. They moved from one old classic to another, until Crispian gradually died out and they were listening to Sinbad's liquid voice raised in a Spiritual . . .

'. . . *All God's chillun got shoes,*
'*When I get to Heaven, gonna put on them shoes* . . .'

Kay began to get an inkling of what Crispian had in mind.

'*And run all over God's heaven,*
'*Heaven* . . . *heaven* . . .'

The last notes died away into silence. Kay knew better than to speak; she could feel Crispian weighing up words and choosing choice phrases.

'That's a pretty remarkable voice you've got there,' he said casually. 'You ought to do something with it.'

'Aw, shucks,' Sinbad grinned. 'I'll bet you tell that to all the singers.'

'I'm serious.' Crispian tensed. 'I mean it.'

'I'll just bet you do.' Sinbad stretched and leaned back, one arm cradling Jasmine, the other arm behind his head. He gave the impression of being greatly amused. 'Got any suggestions?'

Emma whimpered protestingly in her sleep as Crispian leaned forward. He had, Kay realized, been considering this question for quite a long time.

'You should turn professional.'

'Should I now?' Sinbad laughed. 'Fancy that.'

'You have a gift,' Crispian said. 'You shouldn't waste it.'

'That's what I always tell him,' Elf said. 'It's no use, though. He never listens.'

'Oh, I listen,' Sinbad said. 'I jes' don' do nothin' about it.' He thickened his accent grotesquely. Kay had the feeling that he was playing some private game – mocking at them all.

'It's not as difficult as you might think,' Crispian said. He hesitated, then offered, 'I know a lot of people in the music world. I could introduce you to some of my friends.'

'I was waitin' for that!' Sinbad laughed hugely, awakening Jasmine, who stirred and sat up. Poppy moved over to stand behind his shoulder, radiating hostility at them all.

'Come on, keep goin',' he urged. 'Like, tell me, who do you think I ought to be: another Paul Robeson? Another Harry Belafonte? Or do you reckon I oughta aim at the higher things and sing the lead in *Otello*?'

'You could do any of those things.' The hostility was getting through to Crispian, puzzling him. 'You appear to have a limitless range, and the choice would be yours – '

'How about Rock?' Sinbad challenged. 'How about I glue some sequins on my eyebrows and few other places and head up a Rock Group?'

'You could do that too,' Crispian conceded. 'But I think it would be a shame.'

'You'd rather see me leadin' a new Ink Spots?'

'I'd rather see you solo.' Crispian added quickly, 'If that's what you want.'

'An' what do *you* want? What's your angle in all this?'

'I don't have an angle,' Crispian said. 'Not as such. Of course, if you wanted me to, I could look after the business side, make sure you connected with the right people, appeared at the right places – '

'Oh, Whitey, Whitey.' Sinbad was laughing again. 'I been waitin' for this. I knew the pitch was comin', sure as Fate. I jes' didn' know from what direction.'

'I don't understand.' Even in the darkness, Kay could see that Crispian was more red than white at the moment. 'What do you mean?'

'Mean? What you think I mean, white boy? What it sound like?' Sinbad widened his eyes and rolled them, the whites gleaming frighteningly.

'Oh, yassa, Massa. Thank you kindly, Massa. This pore ole woolly head ain't never had no thought in it never. Shore is kind o' you to – '

'Stop it!' Poppy said shrilly. 'Stop it!' She struck him on the back of his neck. 'I hate it when you talk like that! You've been to college, you know you have.' She glared across at Crispian, shaking with rage. 'Don't make him be like that!'

'You sure pack one helluva punch, kid.' Sinbad rubbed the back of his neck ruefully. 'You know that?'

'I don't care!' Poppy was close to hysteria. 'You stop talking like that!' She raised her hand again.

'Okay, okay.' He flinched away, not altogether jokingly. 'Cool it!'

What a pity Marjorie had left, Kay reflected. She would

have found the incident fascinating.

'College, eh?' Crispian said into the sudden silence. 'Which one?'

'Doesn't matter.' Sinbad shrugged. 'Suffice to say I climbed up into the branches of the Ivy League – one of their token Blacks. Yeah, I even graduated. With honours.'

'Then why – ?'

'I just couldn't see goin' through life being everybody's token Black. Oh, there were offers – plenty of them. All kinds. Banking to politics. Everybody was pretty hot on gettin' me into politics back then. Of course, there were some who wanted to see me go on stage, or go up against Muhammad Ali. I tell you, the world is our oyster, us token Blacks. If we want to play the game your way.'

'And you didn't?'

'I wanted to be my own man. See the world. Think things over. Decide what I really wanted to do. If anything.' Sinbad shrugged.

'And – ?'

'I'm still thinking.'

'Isn't it time you came to a decision?'

'Like making you my business manager?' Sinbad leaned back cautiously. Poppy put her arm around his neck and leaned against him. Jasmine looked up at him still half asleep, not certain what was happening, but feeling safe because she was in his arms.

Crispian took a deep breath. 'You could do worse.'

'Maybe I could. But why should I do anything at all? I got a nice quiet life. What do I need with all that hassle?'

'A lot of people would like to be famous – '

'Not me, man!' Sinbad's laugh interrupted him. 'I know who I am. I don't need nobody else to know it.'

'And it would mean money,' Crispian continued relentlessly. 'A lot of money.'

'Money?' Sinbad laughed again. 'Man, didn't you

hear me? I got as much as I can eat. I got a nice soft berth on a good ship. I got all the clothes I can wear, all the air I can breathe, all the friends I want. What do I need with money?'

'With the kind of money you could make,' Crispian spoke quietly but clearly, every syllable reverberating on the still night air, 'with that kind of money, you could buy a yacht. A ship big enough to carry all your family and friends. You could sail around the world. You could sail to all those far-off islands. You could keep your promises.'

Sinbad stopped laughing. Reluctantly, half-fearfully, he looked down into Jasmine's shining face, then turned slowly to encounter Poppy's brilliant hopeful eyes.

'Whitey,' he said softly, 'that one was below the belt. Way, way below the belt.'

CHAPTER XVI

After three days, Kay decided that she had been sent to Coventry. She also decided she was not going to stand for it.

True, absorbed by her own problems, it had taken her a couple of days to notice it. Having capitulated, Sinbad had regained his good humour and begun working with Crispian on a choice of songs for the proposed album. This meant, of course, they were constantly in and out of each other's houses. So, inevitably, was Elf.

Attempts to discourage her were useless, the more subtle going over her head; the more direct prohibited by Crispian's attitude. Not that the direct would work, either. If Elf had not been born with the hide of a rhinoceros, then years of squatting had grown one. She had no sense of wrongdoing; she lived for the moment. The way she had moved into the Norris house had already been forgotten – by her – and it was obvious that she now regarded the place as her own, as surely as if she had bought and paid for it.

'Be nice to Elf,' Crispian had directed. 'Humour her. We don't want to do anything that might upset Sinbad.'

'I'm not so sure he'd be upset.' Kay had intercepted an occasional ironic glance from Sinbad to Elf which suggested that any power Elf might have had to upset him was long since in the past. Nevertheless, Elf was still the mother of his child and he was living in the same house with her. It was possible that Crispian was right.

Kay had settled for treating Elf with a polite indifference which no more discouraged her than saying 'Shoo' to a stray mongrel would have done.

Elf understood nothing less than a door slammed in her

face, and she was accustomed to that.

The slam of Sylvia's front door was still reverberating on the quiet air of the Crescent when Elf tapped at Kay's kitchen door and slipped inside without waiting for an answer. She was carrying an empty cup.

'I thought I wouldn't bother you,' she announced. 'So I went to see if I could borrow a cup of sugar from Rupert's mother, but she didn't answer me.' Elf shrugged. 'I guess she's in a bad mood today.'

'She probably is.' Kay winced inwardly. Finding Elf on her doorstep would be guaranteed to throw Sylvia into a bad mood. It was hard to imagine anything that might induce a worse mood.

'Oh, well, most of the people around here are nice and friendly.' Elf cut her losses. 'The men, anyway. I think men tend to be friendlier than women anyway, don't you?'

'That depends on the circumstances,' Kay evaded. She could not think of any circumstances in which the women of Crozier Crescent would be prepared to welcome Elf and her brood.

Unless – she thought of one – an enterprising husband thought it worthwhile to cultivate them as an adjunct to his latest get-rich-quick scheme. But, given Sinbad's voice, this scheme had a chance of succeeding. So here she was, being friends with Elf. She was sliding into a bad mood herself, and decided she did not like herself very much today.

'Anyway – ' Elf set the empty cup down on the table. 'I hate to bother you again, but Sinbad's gone off with Crispian and I haven't time to go down to the shops, so perhaps *you* could lend me a cup of sugar. I hate to keep bothering you – '

'Quite all right,' Kay said acidly. She took the sugar from the cupboard. 'We're all going to be rich together, aren't we?'

'That's right.' Elf brightened. 'It will be wonderful.'

'It will change a lot of things.' Kay measured out the sugar and returned the box to the cupboard. Forcing a smile, she held the filled cup out to Elf. With any luck, Elf would take it and go.

'I'll say.' Elf ignored the offered cup, settling down for a chat. 'I've been thinking of some of the changes I want to make. We don't really need the kitchen and dining-room as two separate rooms. It's a waste of space. I thought I'd have the wall knocked down and – '

The cup of sugar crashed to the floor from Kay's nerveless fingers.

'Oh dear.' Elf looked down at it mournfully. 'That's too bad. It was part of a nice set, too.' She stooped.

'I'll clear it up,' Kay said.

'All that sugar wasted, too.' Elf stirred it with a forefinger. 'You'll never be able to get all the splinters out of it.'

'I'll let you have another cup,' Kay said between clenched teeth.

'Maybe you've got a plastic cup you could use for it,' Elf suggested helpfully. 'I always made the kids use plastic cups when they were too young to be trusted with good stuff.'

Kay was already in a bad mood when she set out for shopping that afternoon. It was not improved by meeting Sylvia and Alice in the High Street.

It was plain that Sylvia would have swept past, but Alice hesitated uncertainly.

That was when Kay realized abruptly that she had not seen any of the neighbours – except Elf and Marjorie – since the night of the barbecue. And that it had not been mere happenstance.

'I haven't seen you for quite a while,' she hailed Alice, the weaker link.

'Oh!' Guiltily, Alice looked from Kay to Sylvia's obdurate face and back to Kay again, but she did not have it in her to be so unyielding. 'Hello, Kay,' she said.

'Come along, Alice.' Sylvia took her arm. 'We mustn't be late.'

'Sorry – ' Alice smiled apologetically at Kay. 'We have to get to – to – ' Her invention failed her. She glanced hopefully at Sylvia.

'We *don't* have to explain our actions,' Sylvia said emphatically. 'Besides, I'm sure your friend – ' she looked through Kay – 'has important errands of her own.' Kay felt herself receding beyond the pale.

'That's right.' Kay met the challenge head-on. 'I want to buy some more sugar.'

'Yes.' Sylvia quivered and could not resist it. 'It must be expensive, supplying the neighbours.'

'Oh dear.' Alice stepped towards Kay, forgetting that Sylvia still grasped her arm. She was pulled up sharply.

'Now you're being *too* silly!' It was Sylvia's mistake. Alice shook free of her restraining hand and continued her forward movement. 'Kay has the right to entertain anyone she likes in her own home. We all have. If you don't like it, that's too bad, but you ought to try to act like an adult about it.'

'Well!' Sylvia gasped, not having expected mutiny from this usually amenable quarter.

'It's awkward.' Kay restricted her apology to Alice. 'But Crispian has managed to involve himself in a business deal with Sinbad and there's nothing I can do. I *have* to be nice to her.'

Sylvia quivered again, but could not lower herself to ask for details. However, she did not move away.

'Business deal?' Alice looked vaguely alarmed. 'Is that wise? I shouldn't think Crispian could have anything in common with any of *them*.'

'It's all rather speculative – ' Kay was aware that she

might have said too much. Crispian had not asked her to keep it a secret, but he might simply have assumed that she would. Until contracts had been drawn up and everything put on a businesslike basis, someone else might step in and offer Sinbad a more enticing prospect.

'It would *have* to be,' Sylvia snapped. Having broken her own ice, she continued, 'And *Sinbad*! What's his real name? Have you found that out yet?'

'No.' Kay was not going to admit that Crispian had tried but, having been told, 'Sinbad's good enough', had decided that it was, that it might even be a useful gimmick.

'He probably has a record,' Sylvia said. 'We could find it, if we knew his real name.'

'Oh, Sylvia, you shouldn't say things like that.' Alice looked around anxiously to see if they had been overheard. 'I'm sure that's actionable.'

'People who live in glass houses . . .' Sylvia sniffed. 'Especially other people's houses . . .'

Unerringly, Sylvia had put her finger on another of the points bothering Kay. *Why* was Sinbad so concerned to keep his real name concealed? Some dark secret in his past? Or protection for his future if anyone ever dug over the flower-beds again?

She had been successful in putting that thought out of her mind for the past few days. But Elf had triggered it off again this morning when she spoke so casually of knocking down a wall in the Norris house. Surely not even Elf would think she could get away with that. Not unless she had good reason to feel that there would be no repercussions from the real owners.

'I don't think we ought to stand here talking like this,' Alice said fearfully. 'Not right out in the *open* – '

'You may be right,' Sylvia conceded. 'Come back and have a cup of tea – ' She included Kay in the invitation. Hostilities were evidently to be suspended in the interests of getting the latest news. If ever curiosity killed a cat, it would surely kill Sylvia.

'Why not come back to my place?' Kay offered.

'No,' Sylvia vetoed. 'We could be . . . interrupted.'

They were interrupted anyway.

'Jeremy!' Sylvia set down the teapot with a small clatter. 'What are you doing home at this hour?'

'Aha!' Jeremy swayed in the doorway. '"When shall we three meet again", eh? "How now, you secret, black and midnight hags?" Sorry.' He rubbed a hand across his forehead. 'Wrong order. Should have been the other way around.' He frowned. 'Or should it?'

'Jeremy.' Sylvia's lips tightened. 'Answer me!'

'Certainly.' Jeremy blinked at her owlishly. 'Could I have the question again, please? I seem to have mislaid the original somewhere.'

'What . . .' Sylvia enunciated carefully, 'are . . . you . . . doing . . . home? . . . At . . . this . . . hour?'

'Good as any other hour, isn't it?' Jeremy advanced into the room with careful steps. 'Been overworking. Overtired. Putting in fourteen- fifteen-hour days. Got some time coming to me – ' He was shading into belligerency.

'Agency owes me time. Not a machine. Had a heavy business lunch. Very heavy. Working my head to the bone. Bloody clients. Finished late and realized – thought – '

Realized he was too drunk to risk going back to the office. Even his office.

Kay and Alice crossed glances and looked hastily away. Alice found a wrinkle in her skirt and began smoothing it out. Kay concentrated on the teapot.

'Took a taxi. Came home,' Jeremy finished. 'Let them whistle. Not their slave.'

'Why don't you go and lie down?' Sylvia suggested

icily. 'We can discuss this later.'

'Nothing to discuss. Subject finished,' Jeremy said firmly.

Sylvia's flashing eyes disagreed, but she turned back to her guests. 'More tea?' she asked smoothly, lifting the teapot.

'What are we drinking, eh?' Jeremy took the teapot away from her and sniffed at it. 'Tea. *Tea?* That's no good. Let me beef it up a bit for you – ' He headed for the bar, taking the teapot with him.

'No, really,' Alice fluttered nervously. 'It's only four o'clock.'

'Jeremy!' Sylvia snarled.

'What is this prejudice you all have against four o' clock?' Depositing the teapot on the bar, Jeremy turned back to discuss it with Alice. 'Perfectly good hour. Never heard anything said against it before. Innocent as a new-born lamb. Ask anyone. Who's been spreading rumours against it? I'll defend it. To my last breath. Four o'clock is innocent – OK?'

'JEREMY!'

'Everybody is getting overwrought on the subject,' Jeremy complained. He brightened. 'What we all need is a nice little drink.'

'*You've had enough!*'

'Nonsense!' Jeremy drew himself up haughtily. 'Stuff – ' he encountered Sylvia's steely eye – 'and nonsense,' he finished limply.

'I think we ought to be going.' Alice tried to struggle to her feet from the depths of the overstuffed enveloping sofa.

'*Sit down!*'

Alice fell back into the clutches of the sofa. Jeremy collapsed abruptly into a chair. Even Kay was not sure which one had been addressed.

'I'd suggest you go upstairs.' Sylvia fought for a normal

pitch. 'I don't want Rupert to see you like this.'

It went without saying that she would never forgive him for appearing in front of her friends in such a condition. Kay began to feel very sorry for Jeremy.

'Children are tough,' Jeremy said. 'Rupert can take it.' But he got to his feet. 'Little thing like this wouldn't bother any of the children across the way. Why should Rupert be any different?'

'Rupert *is* different,' Sylvia said tightly. 'He is better bred and better brought up.'

'Oh, yes – ' Alice blundered. 'I saw you talking to Elf the other day,' she said to Jeremy.

'*What?*'

'Elf? Elf?' Jeremy looked around wildly, scanning the room at knee level. 'What Elf?'

'The children's mother.' Alice saw her error too late. Sylvia was more furious than ever. 'Elf across the way – '

'Oh, *that* Elf,' Jeremy said. He glanced guiltily at Sylvia and looked away quickly, perhaps noticing that her hands were clenched.

'She and, er, her friend, were out in the front talking to Crispian,' he tried to explain. 'Couldn't just walk past and cut old Crispian dead, could I?'

'Why not?' Sylvia's sideways glare at Kay informed her that it was all her fault. *Once you let the barriers down* . . .

'Well, *you* could,' Jeremy said. 'But I couldn't. Naturally, I had to say hello to him. One word led to another. The rest of them joined in – ' He spread his hands apologetically.

'No way I could have avoided it,' he pleaded with Sylvia.

She gazed at him stonily until his hands dropped by his side and he turned away.

'Perhaps I'll go upstairs and rest for a while,' he said.

'*Do* that,' Sylvia agreed. She watched him leave the room and then went and retrieved the teapot.

'More tea?' She took up smoothly where she had been interrupted.

'No, thank you,' Alice said. 'I've had enough. Oh! I mean – ' She broke off, floundering helplessly.

'We ought to be getting home,' Kay rescued her, although mainly interested in escape for herself.

'That's right,' Alice seconded eagerly. 'Time to start preparing dinner for all my boys.' She laughed nervously. 'I have a full house, you know. And we've taken to eating early because of Barnaby. So much easier than trying to prepare two separate meals – '

'I understand,' Sylvia said. Her smile was a trifle strained.

It would have been subtler to have waited a few more minutes before taking their leave, but they were feeling a trifle strained themselves.

'Why don't you come over for coffee tomorrow morning?' Alice tried to soften their leavetaking. 'I'll see if Candy and Marjorie can drop over, too. We haven't had one of our morning get-togethers for *ages*.'

'Actually,' Sylvia said, 'there was something I wanted to tell you – '

Something crashed to the floor upstairs and she stiffened.

'On second thought – ' She saw them to the door. 'There's no reason it can't wait until morning.'

As the door closed behind them, Kay felt a renewed sympathy for Jeremy.

CHAPTER XVII

Alice had Norman standing by to take Emma and Rupert to the park with Barnaby. Although, in practice, this would probably turn out to mean a walk down to the pub, where the children would cluster outside with orange juice and packets of crisps handed out to them while Norman had a drink inside. The children would be amused and occupied either way, and the adults were free to have a gossip session uninhibited by small ears.

Marjorie was plainly in her most analytical mood; all that was missing was the notebook. She had seated herself just slightly apart from the others so that she could observe everything, with them but not of them and obviously determined to remain so. Kay wondered what she was really thinking and then decided that she would rather not know.

Kay, too, found herself slightly apart from the others, but not from deliberate choice. The others had congregated together defensively and she was considered, if not the enemy, then one not wholly sympathetic to their cause.

Or perhaps it was that she did not have as much at risk as they did. She remembered that Candy had cleared Crispian of nocturnal visits to the Norris house, and now Crispian was going there openly, accompanied by herself. It left everyone unsure of themselves and of her. They were, however, willing to give her the benefit of the doubt. Most of the time.

'I *do* have news,' Sylvia said. 'But – ' She glanced dubiously at Kay and Marjorie.

'*Good* news?' Alice asked apprehensively. After yesterday's scene, she was braced for further devastating revelations regarding Jeremy.

'Very good – ' Sylvia regarded Kay warily. 'But I'll have to swear you all to silence about it.'

'Secrets!' Candy said gleefully. 'Just like school! *I'll* promise. Come on, tell us!'

Sylvia hesitated, transferring her gaze from Kay to Marjorie. '*Everyone* will have to promise – '

'I'll promise,' Alice tried to laugh. 'If you'll promise that it *is* good news.'

'I've told you it is,' Sylvia said, turning back to Kay. 'Well?'

'All right,' Kay said. 'I'll promise, but I agree with Alice. It had better be good.'

'I'll promise too.' Marjorie's voice had a faintly humouring quality that made Sylvia glance at her mistrustfully again.

'Well . . .' Sylvia took a deep breath and plunged. 'I've heard from the Norrises! At last!'

Kay went limp with relief. She had not realized quite how much she had been terrifying herself with her private nightmare.

'When?' Kay pitched her voice over the excited babble. 'What was the date on the letter?'

'It arrived yesterday,' Sylvia said. 'It was dated six days ago and posted in Tobago on their way to Haiti. They say they're island-hopping to gather material for a book on Caribbean local folk festivals. As soon as they've covered the last festival on their schedule, they'll fly back. They can't come earlier because these festivals are once-a-year events and they have a deadline on their book with some of the chapters pre-sold to travel magazines.'

'Thank heavens!' Kay said fervently. The newly-turned earth in the garden was just that, then. The Norrises were safe and well.

'You surprise me,' Sylvia said. 'I didn't think you cared. In fact,' she added, 'I was afraid you might be on the side of your new friends.'

'Oh, really, Sylvia!' Kay protested.

'That *is* good news,' Alice said quickly. 'I'm sure we're *all* very relieved to hear it.'

'But remember – ' Sylvia cautioned. 'No one must breathe a word of it. We don't want *them* to have any advance warning. They might *do* something.'

'What do you imagine they might do?' Marjorie asked in a spirit of scientific enquiry.

'Why – ' Sylvia looked at her in surprise, as though she ought to know. 'They might smash up the furniture, tear out the fixtures – *anything*.'

'That seems a little excessive.' Marjorie smiled disbelievingly. They were left with the impression that she was referring more to Sylvia's imagination than to anything the squatters might do.

'Oh, I don't know.' Kay decided that her relief had been so noticeable that it called for a bit of explanation. Not the main reason, but the secondary one. 'Elf has begun talking about knocking the dining-room wall down over there.'

'She hasn't!' Sylvia gasped, all her worst fears confirmed. (How nice to have such innocent fears.)

'Interesting,' Marjorie annotated. 'She really does live in a world of her own. Total self-absorption and only in minimal touch with reality. I wonder – ' She broke off, the sound of pencils being sharpened almost audible in the silence. Marjorie was going to have another wealth of sociological material at hand when the Norrises arrived to reclaim their property.

'They can't *do* that – ' Sylvia made an instinctive movement towards the door, as though she were going to rush out and try to stop them.

'Oh, she isn't going to do it immediately,' Kay said quickly. 'She's just thinking about it for the future – when they get a bit of money.'

'The future!' Sylvia seemed cheered at the prospect.

'*Their* future is past! The Norrises will be home in less than a month – and that will be the last of *them*.'

'Do you really think it will be that easy, dear?' Alice seemed apprehensive again. 'I mean, *now*?'

'You mean because the Norrises didn't rush back immediately? I shouldn't think so. The Court will understand that they had to cover the Caribbean festivals first.'

'I don't think – ' Marjorie had been watching Alice's face – 'that she meant that.'

'No, I didn't,' Alice said gratefully.

'You mean because they have more than one house? But Crozier Crescent is their main residence and – '

'I didn't mean that, either. I mean, *now* – ' She seemed to despair of being understood and turned to Kay. '*You* must know. She confides in you. How far gone *is* she?'

'Far gone?' Kay looked at her blankly.

'Oh dear,' Alice said. 'Your generation is so outspoken. I keep forgetting I have to translate for you. I mean, how many months pregnant is she?'

'Pregnant!' Sylvia gasped.

'She *can't* be,' Candy wailed.

'I don't see why not,' Alice said. 'It doesn't take brains, you know.'

'Pregnant.' Marjorie nodded with satisfaction, as though another piece of the jigsaw puzzle had just slid smoothly into place.

'She'll have to have an abortion!' Sylvia said decisively.

'Would you like to try telling her that?' Marjorie was openly intrigued to determine just how far Sylvia was prepared to let her hostility carry her.

'It's that black man, of course,' Sylvia ignored the question. 'What else could we expect?'

'Oh no, dear,' Alice contradicted mildly. 'She was

pregnant before he arrived. The early signs were quite unmistakable – if you knew what to look for.'

'Then before she came here – '

'Oh no, dear,' Alice said again.

'It's happened since she began squatting here?' Marjorie asked with the deference of one expert consulting another.

'I'm afraid so,' Alice sighed.

Candy set her coffee cup down with a suddenly shaking hand and sat brooding into its depths.

'Very soon after she got here, I'd say.' Alice sighed again. 'I was hoping Kay might be able to tell us more. I thought Elf might have confided in her.'

'This is the first I've heard about it.' Kay surveyed the others, they all looked as stunned as she felt. With the exception of Marjorie, of course. Her thesis must be shaping up rapidly.

'That *is* a disappointment.' Alice seemed unaware that she had just exploded a bombshell that had reduced Sylvia's news about the Norrises to a damp squib. 'I was so hoping you could tell us something definite.' A little of her coffee spilled on to the table and she noticed that her hands were shaking, too.

'You see,' she said. 'I *would* like to know whether it happened after Norman came home. He's been behaving so strangely lately.'

And if she had to worry about her son, it meant that she needn't worry about her husband. About Arthur – who had been here all along.

'I'm sorry,' Kay said. 'I don't know a thing about it. She's never mentioned it to me.'

'Well . . .' Alice tried to be cheerful. 'I suppose it's something to know that she can be discreet.'

'It's more likely,' Sylvia said, 'that she hasn't even noticed it herself yet. She's a disorganized slut.'

'Perhaps she doesn't think it's worth mentioning.' Candy showed her own claws. 'It's nothing new with her, is it?'

'I'm sorry,' Alice apologized into the brooding silence that followed the last remark. 'I'm being a very bad hostess. Would anyone like any more coffee?'

'No, thank you.' Candy stood up, still brooding. 'I think I ought to be getting home now.'

'Yes.' Sylvia got up too. 'I think I ought to write to the Norrises again. Perhaps they could find a way to come home earlier. After I've warned them about their dining-room wall,' she added, fooling no one but herself.

Marjorie rose reluctantly, seeing her fieldwork slipping away from her. It was probably moments like this when she envied statisticians, archæologists, and others whose raw material could be depended upon to stay put.

Was it by chance or a bit of fancy footwork that Kay found herself going out the door with Marjorie slightly ahead of the others? They strolled along together and Kay noticed that no one tried to catch up with them. Marjorie looked back over her shoulder before she spoke.

'In a hurry?'

'Not really,' Kay said. 'I thought I'd go along to the pub and collect Emma. Her boredom threshold is rather low and I imagine she'll have had enough of standing around outside waiting for Norman to decide it's time to bring them back.'

'I'll come with you, if I may. I find I usually need a long walk to clear my head after close encounters with some of our neighbours – and their thinking.'

'Sylvia can't help it,' Kay said. 'It's the way she's made. Born that way and then early conditioning, I suppose you'd say.' Immediately, she wished she hadn't said that. Experts always loathed it when a layman tried to instruct them in their own field – and she'd probably got it all wrong, anyway.

'I suppose I would.' Marjorie did not seem to mind. Or was it just that she was thinking of something else?
'It's the unconscious level I find especially fascinating,' Marjorie mused aloud. 'That instinctive enmity Sylvia feels for Elf. She hates her without either knowing or understanding the real reason for it. She rationalizes it, yet it's pure instinct.'
'I suppose she sees Elf as some kind of threat.' Kay looked back over her own shoulder. They had left Crozier Crescent and were walking down Mitre Lane, no one else in sight. It was safe to dissect the others freely. 'She and Jeremy have worked hard for everything they have – and then Elf just walks in and, by usurping someone else's home, has everything they have. Really, you can't blame Sylvia for the way she feels.'
'But you don't feel that way about it?'
'In a way, I do. But there can't be many like Elf. As you said, I think she's an isolated case. Sooner or later, the Norrises will come home and get rid of her. I can't see that there's all that much to worry about. Now that we know she isn't going to bring in hordes of other squatters and try to take over the neighbourhood.'
'I see,' Marjorie said. 'Social anarchy: is it infectious or can it be contained?'
Kay remained silent, not sure whether Marjorie was making a comment or trying out a sub-heading. She had the disquieting feeling that Marjorie knew a lot more about everything than she had so far divulged.
Something Marjorie had said – or almost said – a moment ago was nagging at the fringes of her consciousness.
'What did you mean – ?' she began.
'Here we are,' Marjorie said briskly. 'And here's Emma waiting for us, just as you thought she'd be.'
Emma looked up brightly at their approach and skipped to meet them. It was an end to all half-formed speculations.

CHAPTER XVIII

Kay hated keeping secrets from Crispian but felt she had no option this time. He did not want Elf and Sinbad disturbed, and might pass the secret on to them to prevent this. What would be their reaction upon learning that the owners of their dwelling were on their way (leisurely though it might be) towards dispossessing them?

Apart from which, she had the distinct impression that there were a few secrets Crispian was keeping from her at the moment. It must be very expensive to produce an album. What did a set of arrangements, a backing group, a recording session, cost? Where was the money coming from? Did Sinbad have that kind of money? Crispian did not – but he had legal title to a house he could use as collateral for a loan. If the whole thing failed, what would happen to her and Emma? And to Crispian? Was he considering that at all?

She didn't ask the questions because she didn't want to know the answers. In his turn, Crispian was politely incurious about the problems she was facing with her friends now that he was spending so much time with the interlopers; giving, as it were, his imprimatur to them and their activities.

As it was, she was on edge this afternoon, reminding herself that she must not betray by the flicker of an eyelash the information she had received from Sylvia this morning.

Not that Crispian and Sinbad were paying any attention to her. They were too elated by the events of the day thus far. It was only when she carried the tea-tray in to them that they became slightly subdued. (Was it her presence casting the pall? How much *was* Crispian spending on this enterprise?)

'Sit down.' Sinbad took the tray from her hands. 'Join us. Haven't seen you for a while. How are you doing?'

It was a question Kay did not want to go into. 'How are *you* doing?' she countered with a smile. 'That's the important thing.'

'Comin' along pretty well,' Sinbad said. 'We oughta be able to start recording next week.'

'That's marvellous!' She hadn't realized things were moving so fast. 'And how long will it take you to finish?' That was the crux of the matter. If the whole recording could be out of the way by the time the Norrises returned, then it wouldn't matter how upset the squatters got.

'Depends how it goes. If we're lucky, maybe a week. If not – ' He shrugged. 'Better not take too long, though. It costs to hire a recording studio. Even a little bitty private one like Cris's friend is letting us have at a special rate.'

'It shouldn't take more than a week,' Crispian said hastily, almost guiltily. (How much money had he sunk into this venture?) 'You're good, the session musicians are good, the recording equipment is the best. What could possibly go wrong?'

'Gremlins, man, gremlins!' Sinbad grinned hugely. 'Aren't they an English speciality?'

Or an Elf. Kay just stopped herself from saying it aloud. Something of the disturbance she felt must have shown in her face, however, for Sinbad's smile faded and Crispian began to frown.

'We're only kidding around, honey,' Sinbad said. 'Nothing's going to go wrong. We'll have the whole album wrapped up and ready for merchandising before you know it. Then the money will start rolling in.' He grinned at Crispian. 'So they tell me.'

'I'm not worried about that,' Kay lied gallantly.

'Then suppose you tell Old Sinbad just what the problem is. You're worried about something, I can tell.

White woman, black woman – ' he looked at Crispian – 'it's the same all over the world. They get that expression on their face and we're all in for it. All us menfolk.'

Crispian was still frowning, but there was no reason why she should not unburden at least a portion of the problem. Especially when Sinbad might be able to do something about it.

'I've been talking to Elf – ' she began.

'Oh-oh.' Sinbad seemed to have an idea of what was coming next. 'Go on.' He regarded her warily.

'She's making plans – ' Kay tried to ignore Crispian, who had moved behind Sinbad's back and was wig-wagging frantic signals to shut up.

'She was telling me she wants to tear down the dining-room wall,' Kay continued. Let Crispian rage at her, she had to say it. 'She can't *do* that, really, she can't. The house *does* belong to the Norrises, after all.'

'Oh, *that*!' Kay had the curious impression that Sinbad was relieved. What had he expected her to say? 'Don't you worry about that. I'll see to it she doesn't do anything like that.'

Yes, but how much longer will you be around to stop her?

'Yes, but – ' Kay tried to frame the question delicately.

'They're your laws, lady.' Sinbad shook his head. 'I didn't believe our Elf when she told me. But I checked up and, sure enough, she was right. She could move into just about any empty house she fancied and live there like she owned it. It might not be exactly moral, but it sure as hell isn't exactly illegal, either. You can call picking up a five-pound note in the street "stealing by finding", but you let anybody who wants to walk into an unoccupied house and set up housekeeping. They're *your* laws, and I hope you understand them, because I sure as hell don't!'

'There are a lot of ancient laws still on the Statute Books,' Crispian tried to explain. 'In recent years, people realized what they could mean in present-day life and began taking advantage of them.'

'Most people would never dream of doing such a thing,' Kay said.

'Most people.' Sinbad was still shaking his head slowly. 'If there is one thing I can guarantee you, it's that Elf isn't most people. No man. That lady is something else again.'

'But you can control her.' Kay tried not to sound too eager. 'If you can keep her from tearing the wall down – '

'That's just about all I can do,' Sinbad said. 'So don't get any fancy ideas that I could persuade her to move out and go away. She likes it here.'

'I'm sure Kay didn't mean anything of the kind – ' Crispian began.

'Relax, man,' Sinbad said. 'You think I don't know we aren't the most desirable neighbours in the world? I'm not blaming you. If I were in your shoes, I wouldn't like it either. But where else has she got to go? This is the softest berth she's ever found and, for the kids' sakes alone, I hope she'll hang on to it just as long as she can.'

'Where *did* she live before?' Kay asked curiously. The answer might give some clue as to how Elf had discovered the Norris house was empty and available. As Sylvia had pointed out, Crozier Crescent was not a place one could stumble over easily.

'Live? Anywhere and everywhere. Always on the move. Used to take me the first two or three days of every leave, trying to track her down. She never believed in writing letters. She'd leave messages for me with the neighbours. Which would have been okay, except that half the time the neighbours had moved on or been busted by the cops. One time a couple of years ago, it took me a whole week to catch up with her.'

'I'm surprised you bothered,' Kay muttered. It was an echo of Sylvia; she recognized it as such and wished she hadn't said it.

'Don't get the wrong idea. It wasn't because of her. That was over a long time ago.' His face was sombre. 'But that little Jasmine-blossom is mine and I'm not letting her go down the drain. I'm not running out on my responsibility –' He looked at Kay challengingly. 'Not like some white boys I could mention. My kid knows she's got a daddy and she knows who her daddy is!'

'If you feel like that,' Kay said, 'I'm surprised you don't try to get custody and take her back to the States with you.'

'Oh, lady, lady – ' Sinbad gave a pained chuckle. 'Maybe I might, if I could figure out a good way to explain her to my wife and my twin boys. Yeah – ' He nodded wryly. 'Our Elf likes the married ones. Haven't you cottoned on to that yet?'

'I'm sorry,' Kay said. 'I didn't mean – '

'It's all right. I know what you meant. But it's better for a little girl to be with her mother and Elf isn't all that bad. I've known her for a long time. There isn't what there used to be between us, but there's still a powerful fondness. I suppose I feel kinda like *her* father, too. She could use one.

'First she was searching for her identity. Then she joined the Flower Power Children. Then she was doing her thing. After that, she let it all hang out. Now she's trying to get her head together.' He sighed heavily.

'Ain't no way she's gonna get it all together.' This time the heavy accent was not mockery, rather it had the sound of a sad and solemn verdict handed down by elders in his family who spoke that way.

The doorbell rang sharply, startling them.

'Oh-oh, speak of the devil,' Sinbad said with sudden prescience as Kay went to answer it. He was right.

Elf stood there, flanked by Poppy and Jasmine. 'Is Sinbad here?' she asked.

'Come in.' Kay stepped back, viewing Elf with more

sympathy since Sinbad's rundown on her. She had been thinking of Elf as a predator, suddenly she seemed a victim. Elf had thrown herself into every passing phase of the Permissive Society and was now stranded on the sands after that high tide had receded. An anachronism without knowing it. She, and the children with her, were the detritus of the Permissive Society.

'I thought they'd be back from town now.' Elf followed her into the living-room. Jasmine detached herself from her mother's side and went to her father.

'Hello, honey.' Sinbad patted her head. He and Crispian had both risen when Elf came into the room, an exaggerated courtesy, perhaps prompted by guilt since they had just been talking about her.

Kay watched Elf cross the room, hoping desperately that Alice was wrong. But there was no doubt that Elf's billowing gown did not billow quite so much as it had a few weeks ago. To her horror, Elf turned suddenly and caught her staring.

'I wondered who was going to be the first to notice,' Elf said, lowering her bulk on to the sofa beside Sinbad.

'Actually, it was Alice.' Since there was apparently going to be no pretence about it, Kay decided she was not going to take the blame alone. Crispian was annoyed enough with her already.

'I always show early.' Elf laughed comfortably. 'I'm huge for months beforehand and people always get nervous thinking it's due any minute.' She sounded as though she thought it were a lovable attribute to have.

There was no love on Sinbad's face. There was shock, consternation, and something that shaded into the unreadable as his eyes went blank.

Poppy's face looked pinched and ancient with a sudden bleak despair. It was news to her, too.

Crispian pursed his lips in a soundless whistle, while his expression became abstracted. What effect – if any –

would this have on his plans?

Only Jasmine remained unaffected. It had all gone over her head.

The atmosphere hummed with unasked questions, but Elf did not notice. Her mind had skipped to more vital topics.

'I thought I'd better come and get you,' she said to Sinbad. 'Something's gone wrong with the kitchen sink. It's making awful glopping noises and spitting up stinking water and all sorts of strange bits and pieces.'

'Oh-oh.' Sinbad got up rapidly.

'I think maybe the baby threw something she shouldn't have down the garbage disposal,' Poppy said. 'I tried to watch her. Honestly I did – ' She was on the verge of tears, perhaps of hysteria. 'But I can't watch her every single minute. I can't!' The tears came with a rush.

'Okay, okay.' Sinbad picked her up, comforting her. 'Nobody's blaming you. Take it easy. These things happen.' He started for the door, carrying her. Poppy dropped her head on to his shoulder, still sobbing heartbrokenly.

Elf remained on the sofa, smiling serenely, as though the whole thing had nothing to do with her.

'You coming?' At the door, Sinbad turned back to her.

'You can manage,' she said, leaning back.

'Listen, lady – ' For the first time, Sinbad was close to losing his temper. 'It's your house, your kids, your . . . mischief! You come along!'

With a smile to Kay for the incomprehensible whims of men, Elf shrugged and got up slowly and followed him from the house.

'Well, well, well,' Crispian said softly. 'Except – ' he met Kay's eyes – 'it's not at all well, is it?'

CHAPTER XIX

Ever since the barbecue, Emma had been agitating for a tea-party of her own. Thank goodness the weather was keeping fair so that it could be held out of doors. Alice had agreed to let Barnaby attend and, after a great deal of pressure on Rupert's part, Sylvia had allowed Rupert to come – albeit with frequent trips to the window to keep an eye on him.

Having brought out the tea-trolley piled with little sandwiches and cakes, Kay retreated to the kitchen where she only half-listened to the childish voices drifting through the open windows.

'I've just about decided what kind of dog I want.' Emma was getting to be a first-class bore on the subject. The sooner she actually got the dog, the better. 'I'll get it on my birthday in October. Only two more months.'

'My birthday came in May,' Rupert said. 'I'm eleven years old already. Maybe my father will give me a dog for Christmas.'

His father would be more likely to give him a pink elephant, the way things were going. Kay wiped the smile off her face; it wasn't really a laughing matter. It was too bad Sylvia didn't devote more time to worrying about that instead of worrying about the squatters. Or perhaps she had decided upon the squatters as the lesser evil to worry over.

'I'll be eleven years old in December.' That was Poppy.

'December is for Christmas.' Emma seemed shocked.

'I know,' Poppy said. 'I wish I was born another month. Everybody tells me my presents are for Christmas *and* my birthday. The other kids get presents twice a year.'

Poor Poppy, short-changed all around.

'I was nine before you came here.' Barnaby struggled to keep his end up. 'I'll be ten next February.'

'I'll be nine in March,' Jasmine said.

In a few more years, they would probably identify themselves by astrological signs. It was surprising they didn't already do so. Could there have been one fad Elf had missed out on? Or were they so bored by their mother's enthusiasms that they were ignoring them in a natural reaction?

'Aha! What have we here?' The deep bass note brought Kay to the window.

'A party, as I live and breathe!' Jeremy stood by the tea-trolley, swaying gently as was his wont these days.

'So it is.' Crispian was right behind him. 'Why don't we go inside and see if we can beg a cup of tea from Kay? Or coffee.'

Kay left the window and went out to lend support, if necessary.

'You're home early,' she greeted Crispian. 'I wasn't expecting you so soon.'

'Ran into old Jeremy, here.' Crispian smiled at the children. 'He offered me a lift home and I thought it would be a good idea.' He added softly, 'I drove.'

'Yes, that *was* a good idea,' Kay agreed, equally softly.

'I can phone in my copy later,' Crispian said. 'Meanwhile, why don't we grown-ups stop boring the kids and go in and have a nice cup of black coffee?'

Too late. Sylvia had appeared in her window again and spotted Jeremy. She rapped on the window sharply.

'I think you're being paged,' Kay said.

Both Jeremy and Rupert jumped guiltily and turned towards the window. Poppy turned also. She and Rupert were sitting next to each other – no doubt another reason for Sylvia's surveillance – and they moved in unison. Realizing the summons was not for them, they turned back again with exactly the same expression of relief on their faces. They might have been brother and sister.

'I suppose I'd better go and see what she wants.' Jeremy took an indecisive step forward which brought him, momentarily, to hover over Poppy and Rupert. In that brief instant, the three faces formed a triangle, Jeremy at the apex. When you followed the lines of the triangle, you found a smaller blurred version of his face at each end of the base.

Might have been brother and sister? They *were* brother and sister!

Kay took an involuntary step backwards and encountered the warning pressure of Crispian's hand on her arm.

Jeremy frowned at them, puzzled, then turned as Sylvia rapped on the window-pane again. 'Coming,' he muttered. 'I'm coming.'

'We'll go away too – ' Crispian smiled at the children – 'and leave you to your party.' He opened the back door for Kay.

They entered the kitchen silently and Crispian walked over and carefully closed the windows before turning back to Kay.

'Good God! Did you see what I saw?' He was genuinely shaken.

'I'm afraid so.'

'Then it wasn't my imagination?' Crispian shook his head. 'I was afraid it wasn't. But – good God! – how did he dare? In the same street with his wife? Is he crazy?'

'He *has* been behaving oddly,' Kay said.

Abruptly, Crispian began to chuckle, in the light-hearted way of a man without a pigeon loft of his own watching the horizon darken with his neighbour's pigeons coming home to roost. 'No wonder old Jeremy hasn't drawn a sober breath since they moved in.'

'I don't think it's funny.' But the corners of Kay's mouth began to twitch traitorously. 'If Sylvia finds out, she'll kill him!'

'Only if he's lucky!'

'Oh no!' Kay had been looking out of the window and stopped laughing abruptly. 'He's coming back!'

'Who, Jeremy?' Crispian shouldered her aside to look. 'Good God – you're right!'

Before he could say any more, Jeremy was at the door and inside. He seemed to have sobered up considerably.

'You saw, didn't you?' He gazed at them mordantly. 'Does Sylvia know?'

'I don't think so,' Kay said. 'She couldn't have seen it from the same angle. It was just the way you were all grouped suddenly – and the expression on your faces.'

'The kids don't know?' Jeremy pleaded for reassurance.

'No possible way they could suspect,' Crispian said. 'It requires a certain level of sophistication to think of such a thing.'

'Also,' Kay said, 'Marjorie's made a couple of cryptic remarks. Only to me,' she added hastily, seeing Jeremy's face change. 'Not to Sylvia. I didn't understand them at the time but, when I saw you all standing there together, suddenly they made sense.' No wonder Marjorie had been so fascinated by the subject of instinctive enmity.

'Marjorie!' Jeremy said vindictively. 'Sylvia is right. That woman has too much time on her hands to worry about other people's business. Christ!' He brushed a hand over his forehead. 'I could use a drink!'

'I'll bet you could.' Crispian headed for the drinks cabinet. 'We all could.'

Kay glanced anxiously out of the window, but the children were all happily engaged in their tea-party, unconscious of adult dramas.

'But what made you think you could get away with it?' Crispian handed Jeremy a large double.

'Good Lord!' Jeremy seemed shocked by the question. 'You don't actually imagine I invited her here, do you?'

'Didn't you?'

'Certainly not. I happened to meet her in town a few months ago. Well, it had been years since I'd seen her. We went for a few drinks – old times' sake and all that. Told each other how the world had been treating us. I happened to mention Crozier Crescent – '

It all began to fall into place. Jeremy, unable to resist the temptation to show off, any more than he had been able to resist the temptations strewn in his path during the years when everybody had been trying to live up to the legend of Swinging London; Jeremy, swanking about how well he was doing, with his expensive home, his semi-celebrity neighbours; the eminent music critic next door, the famous husband-and-wife travel writers across the street, who travelled to such exotic places, so often – and for such long trips . . .

'How was I to know the silly cow would take it as an invitation to move in?' Jeremy was aggrieved. 'The thought never crossed my mind. And she didn't say anything about it, or I'd have put a stop to it. I just came home one night – and there she was. I saw her in the window. I slipped over later – after it was dark – and tried to talk sense to her, but she wouldn't budge.'

'So *you're* the one who's been sneaking in there at night – '

'Not me. Not *every* night.' Jeremy denied it vehemently. 'But I had to keep on good terms with her, or I didn't know what she'd do. She's very volatile, you know.' He shuddered. 'She might have told Sylvia.'

'You *do* know she's pregnant again, don't you?' Kay asked curiously.

'No! Oh God, no! It lacked only that!' Jeremy shuddered again, then became aware of their combined measuring gaze.

'It wasn't me!' His voice rose wildly. 'I never laid a finger on her!'

Oddly, Kay believed him. It seemed that once Elf's men were finished with her, they were thoroughly disenchanted. For one reason or another, they might keep in touch – but only metaphorically.

'Oh God! Does Sylvia know?'

'Alice told us all yesterday,' Kay said. 'Sylvia was there with the rest of us.'

'I thought she was in a bad mood last night,' Jeremy said. 'Worse than usual, that is.'

'She didn't take it well.' Kay could offer no honest comfort.

'She wouldn't.'

The telephone began to ring. Kay guessed it would be Sylvia and she was right.

'May I speak to Jeremy, please?'

'Tell her I'm on my way.' Jeremy was already halfway out of the door. 'God! There's no peace anywhere!'

'He's on his way, Sylvia,' Kay said.

'And you can send Rupert along, too,' Sylvia said. 'He's been over there quite long enough.'

'I'll tell him.' Kay was too preoccupied to resent the implication that Rupert risked a nasty infection if he remained any longer. She rang off abstractedly.

'I wouldn't be in Jeremy's shoes for anything.' Crispian was still congratulating himself on his own luck. 'Just wait until Sylvia finds out. And she will. Too many people know now. It's bound to come out. Those kids look too much alike.'

'And especially wait until Sylvia does some mental arithmetic.' Kay had been doing some of her own.

'What do you mean?'

'Do you realize that Poppy is just seven months younger than Rupert?'

It took him a moment to make the connection, then his

eyes widened. 'You mean that while Sylvia was in the last stages of pregnancy, old Jeremy was off on the tiles with Elf? *And* getting her pregnant, as well?'

'Sylvia will kill him,' Kay said. 'She really will.'

'Look on the bright side,' Crispian said. 'There's obviously a lot more to old Jeremy than meets the eye. Maybe the worm will turn the rest of the way and *he'll* kill Sylvia.'

'Even so,' Kay said. 'I don't see him going off into the sunset and living happily ever after with Elf, do you?'

'No,' Crispian said thoughtfully. 'I can't say that I do.'

CHAPTER XX

Morning dawned grey and murky. The sort of morning when one moved at half-speed, rather grateful for the lack of sun with its insidious moral blackmail whispering that one ought not to waste the bright hours indoors. This morning there was not even the temptation to glance out of the windows. The rain would begin falling soon enough, the fine spell was over.

Kay was unprepared for the sudden, urgent voice in her ear when she answered the telephone.

'Don't let Emma out!' Sylvia said urgently. 'Keep her inside. No matter what!'

'What?' Kay was bewildered. If anything, she had expected the next telephone call from Sylvia to be furious, perhaps tearful, but not this.

'I've sent Rupert back to bed,' Sylvia said. 'Poor little devil – he doesn't know what he's done wrong. And I can't explain. It's not him – it's *them*!'

'What have *they* done?' Sylvia did not sound as though she had yet discovered the extent of Jeremy's perfidy. She was still concerned about the paltry iniquities of the squatters.

'Haven't you seen?' Sylvia sounded personally affronted. 'Just go – don't move the curtains – and look out of the window. The police are over there!'

Cautiously, Kay moved towards the window. Sure enough, a police car was parked outside the Norris house. A doctor's car was also there.

'Have the Norrises come back?' she asked.

'Not that I know of. More likely, that ghastly addict has taken an overdose.' Sylvia snorted. 'That sort of thing is always on the cards with that sort of person.'

Even as Kay watched, an ambulance drew up and decanted two men carrying a furled stretcher.

'There!' Sylvia said. 'Did you see that?' Obviously, she was keeping a sharp watch from behind her own curtains.

'What's going on?' Crispian came up behind Kay and looked over her shoulder.

'Trouble, I'm afraid.' Kay covered the receiver with her hand. 'Sylvia rang, but she doesn't know any more about it than we do. She just saw the police car and grabbed for the phone.'

'Keep Emma inside.' Unconsciously, Crispian echoed Sylvia. 'I'll go over and find out what's happening.'

'Kay! Are you still there?' Sylvia called her sharply back to order. 'Where is Crispian going?'

Since Crispian was walking up the Norris path, the answer should have been self-evident.

'He's going to see what's happening.'

'Let me know as soon as he finds out,' Sylvia commanded. 'If only Jeremy weren't at the office, he could go over, too.' Her voice took on a note of complaint. 'Jeremy is never here when one needs him.'

Sylvia was still unsuspecting, then; she would not be so anxious to send Jeremy into the Norris house if she had any idea of the truth. But for how much longer could she be kept in ignorance? Even if she didn't notice the resemblance between Rupert and Poppy, there was always the danger that Jeremy himself might blurt out a confession in a suicidal moment.

'Yes – ' Kay tried to shut off the dangerous thoughts, as though the telephone might somehow transmit them from her mind to Sylvia's. 'Crispian will find out for us.'

Or would he? Kay watched him ring the doorbell and saw the door swing open. But a policeman blocked the entrance. She watched the pantomime continue.

Crispian spoke urgently, ingratiatingly. The policeman

answered politely, adamantly. The policeman had been in this situation before; Crispian had not.

Crispian gestured towards the interior of the house. The policeman shook his head. Crispian appeared to be putting up an argument which stopped abruptly as the policeman motioned him to one side.

The ambulance men came out carrying the stretcher with someone on it. A tall white shape hovered in the background. The policeman moved back inside the house and shut the door while Crispian was still staring after the stretcher.

'What is it?' Sylvia was still on the line. '*Who* is it? Could you see?'

'No.' Kay watched the men load the stretcher into the waiting ambulance.

Crispian, in a somewhat delayed reaction, started down the path towards the ambulance men. They slammed shut the ambulance doors, darted around to the front, leaped in and started the engine. It appeared that they were as versed as policemen in the ways of curious onlookers. Crispian was left on the kerb, watching the ambulance drive away. The blue light was not flashing, neither did they bother to turn on the klaxon. Could it be that there was no reason for urgency?

'I didn't see anything.' Belatedly, Kay realized why. She had been so intent on Crispian that she had barely registered it. 'I couldn't. The head was covered by a blanket.'

Sylvia drew in her breath sharply, then recovered herself. 'Well, it's no more than we expected.' Generously, she included Kay in her forebodings. 'He's dead, I suppose. They usually are, with an overdose.'

'I'll ring you back later,' Kay said. Crispian was heading home, looking grim. She replaced the receiver firmly.

'What is it?' She met Crispian at the door.

'They won't say.' He shook his head. 'But it looks bad. You saw the stretcher?'

'I couldn't see who was on it.'

'Neither could I.' Their eyes met. They moved towards the window. They were in time to see the doctor get into his car and drive away. The police car was still there.

'Dead?' Kay forced herself to ask it.

'Afraid so. They don't cover the face otherwise, do they?'

'Who?'

'Ah, that's the question.' Crispian squinted out, not wanting to pull the curtains aside.

'Sylvia thought . . . Wade?'

'He was in the hallway when they carried the stretcher out.'

Farther down the street, Marjorie's door opened. They watched in silence as Marjorie walked swiftly to the Norris house, rang the bell and was admitted without hesitation.

'One of the children?' Crispian began to pace the floor.

'The body on the stretcher looked too long for a child.' He knew that; he had had a closer view of it than she had. But he didn't want to consider the alternatives.

'Why the hell doesn't someone *tell* us something?' Crispian burst out.

'Perhaps they don't think it's any of our business.' But business was the operative word. Crispian and Sinbad had their business deal all lined up and ready to roll. They'd start recording in a few more days. If anything had happened to Sinbad. . . How much *would* Crispian stand to lose?

There was a knock at the back door. Kay went to answer it while Crispian paced back to the window. He did not appear to have heard it.

'What did Crispian find out?' Kay had expected Sylvia, but it was Norman who stepped into the kitchen asking the question. Norman, looking haggard and distraught, insisting on an immediate answer. 'What happened over there?'

'We don't know,' Kay said. 'The police wouldn't – ' She broke off as, with a disbelieving gesture, he stalked past her into the living-room. She followed him uneasily.

'All quiet,' Crispian reported, without turning. 'If we rang them, do you think the police would answer the phone?'

'We could try, I suppose,' Kay said dubiously. 'But – '

'It's Elf, isn't it?' Norman demanded abruptly. 'It's all my fault. The other two found out about the baby and went mad with jealousy. Which one of them killed her?'

Kay collapsed on to the sofa. Crispian turned to stare at Norman incredulously.

'Hold on a minute. We don't know that anything of the sort has happened.' But there was a faint note of cheer in Crispian's voice. He would rather that something had happened to Elf than to Sinbad.

'Don't we?' Norman faced them defiantly. 'I warned her, but she laughed at me.'

Elf had a point there, Kay thought. It was highly unlikely that either Sinbad or Wade would be consumed with jealousy if Elf were to turn to another man. One had the feeling that, if anything, they would have been relieved. However, Norman obviously felt that he had snatched a prize out from under the noses of great competition. It would be unkind to disillusion him. In any case, the situation had just changed radically.

A car door slammed out in the street. Norman and Crispian reached the window in a dead heat, Kay right behind them. The police were leaving.

'Is there anyone else in the car?' Norman asked. 'Are they taking anyone away?'

'What are you all doing?' Emma appeared in the doorway behind them, visibly puzzled at the sight of three adults huddled around the same window in a manner more fitting to her own equals.

'Nothing.' Crispian gave the answer she would have given had their positions been reversed. 'Why don't you run away and play?'

'Can I go out – ?'

'No! Play upstairs!'

'I'm hungry.' Emma changed tack plaintively. 'Aren't we going to eat today?'

'All right.' With guilty surprise, Kay discovered it was nearly one. 'Come and help me fix some lunch. Norman – ?'

'No, I won't stay, thanks.' His mouth twitched in what might have been meant for a smile. 'I'd better get back. My mother will be wondering where I am.' But he lingered by the window.

Emma followed Kay to the kitchen, still nursing her grievances. '*Why* can't I go out?'

'It's going to rain,' Kay said. 'Besides, no one else is out. You don't want to go out by yourself, do you?'

'Yes,' Emma said.

'Well – ' Kay glanced skywards, the rain could not hold off much longer. 'We'll see after lunch.' Surely it would be raining by then.

Emma also glanced out of the window, but concentrated at ground level and discovered a new grievance.

'Why don't we ever have a barbecue? *They're* having another barbecue. Can't I go over?'

'You haven't been invited.' Kay watched the children trail across the yard to the barbecue. Poppy was wrestling with the sack of charcoal, Jasmine carefully balanced a platter heaped with buns and raw hamburger patties, and (Kay winced) even little Heather carried a handful of knives and forks, holding prongs and blades at a perilous angle.

'Why don't *we* get a barbecue?' Emma demanded.

'Would you rather have a barbecue for your birthday than a dog?' Kay suggested hopefully.

'No,' Emma backtracked instantly. 'I'd rather have a dog. *Anyone* can have a silly old barbecue.'

The children were pale and subdued. Kay watched Poppy struggle to light the charcoal as though her life depended on it. With the same desperate intensity, Jasmine concentrated on splitting the buns. It looked as though someone had told them they must be brave little girls and try not to cry. Only Heather seemed unaware that her world had turned upside down.

The scene blurred as the first drops of rain splattered against the window-pane, but the children worked on doggedly at their tasks.

'It's raining now,' Emma pointed out.

Poppy looked up at the sky defiantly, then snatched rolls and meat from Jasmine, arranging them on the grill over the smoking charcoal. She could never get them cooked in time, the charcoal was not properly alight.

Marjorie came to the back door and called to the children. Only Heather responded, rubbing her hands petulantly over her face to wipe away the rain. Marjorie closed the door behind her, and turned away, obviously expecting the older children to gather up their meal and follow. Marjorie's experience with children was largely academic.

Ignoring the increasingly heavy rain, Poppy poked frantically at the charcoal. If determination could do it, the meat would have been cooked by now.

Jasmine crouched by the barbecue, watching sombrely as the buns began to break up under the impact of the rain and more smoke arose from the charcoal setting her to coughing.

Marjorie came to the door and called again. This time, Jasmine rose slowly and said something to Poppy. Poppy shook her head and Jasmine went back to the house alone.

Poppy refused to admit defeat. It had become a personal

fight between her and the dampening charcoal, as though some kind of order might yet be restored to her shattered world if only she could win this battle.

The rain had intensified into a driving downpour, lashing against the windows, bouncing off the sills like hailstones. Poppy's hair was plastered to her skull, her clothes clung to her small frame; she might have been standing underneath a shower, but she did not appear to notice.

This time it was Sinbad who came to the door. He stood looking out at her, shaking his head sorrowfully, then he opened the door and dashed through the downpour. He caught up the sack of charcoal and spoke to Poppy.

She shook her head stubbornly, still gazing at the grill.

He shrugged helplessly, then picked her up and tossed her over his shoulder, ignoring her struggles to free herself. As the door opened to them, her face contorted – she was crying at last.

Shaken, Kay turned away from the window. There was nothing left to see now. Even the food had disintegrated under the impact of the driving rain, separated and fallen through the grill into the wet charcoal.

Kay blinked tears from her own eyes. Perhaps Elf hadn't been much, but she had been *there*. What would happen to the children now?

CHAPTER XXI

For the rest of the day, rumour and counter-rumour raced round Crozier Crescent. Crispian had taken Norman down to the pub where, considering the state Norman was in, it was quite probable that they started more rumours than they picked up.

Repeated attempts to telephone the Norris house only led to the conclusion that their receiver had been left off the hook. Later, Crispian had slipped over and pushed a note through the letter-box but this too brought no response.

Sylvia's attitude was one of muted triumph: it was not proper to gloat over any death, but there could be no denying that this one was highly satisfactory.

'The police will *have* to do something now,' Sylvia declared. 'They *can't* allow three little girls to stay alone in that house with those men.'

'But the men are their fathers,' Kay protested.

'Well, two out of three.' Crispian was not above twisting the knife. So long as Sylvia was not aware of the reason for it, he was prepared to get a certain amount of enjoyment out of Jeremy's discomfiture.

Without looking at Crispian, Jeremy deliberately helped himself to another three inches of the most expensive whisky. Jeremy had not said a word, other than 'hello', since Sylvia had dragged him over.

'I've sent Rupert to his grandmother,' Sylvia said. 'I put him on the afternoon train and Mother will meet it and collect him. She was delighted. If you're wise, you'll do the same with Emma. There may be scenes around here in the next few days it would be better for a child not to witness.'

Sylvia might be right. Once in a while, she was bound to be. On the other hand, perhaps Sylvia's answers were only right for Sylvia. There was nothing Emma could discover that was even roughly comparable to what Rupert could discover if his father were to crack.

And Jeremy looked very close to a crack-up.

Kay risked a sidelong glance at him. As Crispian had noted, Jeremy had not drawn a sober breath since Elf moved into the Norrises' house. He was not about to endanger his track record now.

Sylvia appeared not to notice. Perhaps she didn't care. Or perhaps that excellent instinct warned her that she would be happier not knowing the reason for Jeremy's breakdown. It was so much more comfortable to blame it on overwork and overtranquillization. (Does the ostrich keep its head in the sand until the very moment that the enemy starts plucking out its tail feathers?)

'It's too bad about Barnaby,' Sylvia said. 'He *is* with his grandmother. I don't suppose Norman's ex-wife – ?'

'She's in South America,' Kay said. 'And I understand she was an orphan.'

'Probably why she was so erratic.' Sylvia dismissed her. 'Still, Barnaby's the youngest. He may not notice anything wrong at all.'

Jasmine and Heather were both younger than Barnaby, but Sylvia wasn't worrying about them. In any case, there was no escape for them.

'Are you sure – ' Sylvia turned to Crispian suspiciously – 'you don't know any more about it? I thought you were as thick as thieves with those people.'

'Sorry.' Crispian shrugged. 'You ought to ask Marjorie. She's been inside over there all day.'

'Marjorie!' It was an imprecation. 'She *would* be! And she never tells anyone anything.'

'Perhaps we can read all about it in her memoirs,' Crispian said. 'In about another thirty years . . .'

Jeremy swayed visibly, encountered the wall and remained propped against it. A large dollop of Scotch splashed from his tilted glass to the carpet.

'I think we ought to be going.' For the first time, Sylvia appeared to notice that all was not quite as it should be with her husband.

'Mmm,' Crispian said, judiciously refraining from urging her to stay longer.

'You *will* let me know what's happened as soon as you find out,' Sylvia directed.

In the morning, the police car was back. It was still raining and looked as though it would continue all day. Alice rang and, with great thankfulness, Kay accepted her offer to take Emma to a matinee with Barnaby. She would take them on to tea afterwards, Alice said, and bring them back in the early evening. She could stand a day out of the house herself, she added. Norman was as cheerful as a funeral and Arthur wasn't much better. It would be a good thing when all this was over and the neighbourhood was back to normal.

What did Alice consider normal? The days when Elf had been a live nuisance, or the earlier time before Elf had appeared on the scene at all. Possibly Alice didn't know herself.

Anyway, it meant that she and Crispian could have a quiet afternoon until he left to cover the evening performance at the Royal Festival Hall. It would be nice to be able to have a conversation that didn't have to take place in hushed tones because of listening little ears.

And thank heavens for that, was all Kay could think when Sinbad appeared at the front door shortly after Emma had left.

'Okay if I come in for a few minutes?' he asked. 'I'm aching to have a few words on a reasonably adult level. They do their best over there, but you can't have much of a conversation with a spaced-out freak and three little girls.'

'Come in, come in.' Crispian almost snatched him inside. 'You're welcome here any time. You know that.'

'I thought Marjorie was over there with you,' Kay said.

'She's giving a lecture today. She's been great, but people have their own lives. You can't impose on them indefinitely.'

It was not a point of view Elf would have recognized. Kay wondered what it portended for the future. And for the Norrises.

'We saw the police car over there again this morning,' Crispian said.

'Oh, man!' Sinbad sank into a chair, hitching it around slightly so that he would be able to keep an eye on the Norris house. 'I can't believe it. Life wasn't bad enough. They had to throw that at us.'

'What happened?' Kay asked.

'You don't know?' He shook his head. 'I wish I could say that.'

'We know it was Elf,' Crispian said.

'Yeah,' Sinbad sighed deeply. 'It was Elf. My little Jasmine came running to me yesterday morning and said she couldn't wake her Mummy up. I went in and Elf was lying there with her face sort of in the pillow – but she always used to sleep face down half the time. Shouldn't have mattered. But I turned her over and she was dead. I tried the kiss of life while Wade called the doctor – ' He shuddered. 'But it wasn't any use.'

'The police came,' Crispian said.

'Sure, they came. She was a healthy woman, prime of life, and – ' he grinned wryly – 'it wasn't as if she'd been taking the Pill. They wanted to know what happened. So did I. They – they took her away to find out.'

'And the police came back this morning,' Crispian prodded as Sinbad came to a halt and sat brooding.

'Yeah, they came to me. They'll come to you, too. They're gonna be doing the rounds. Because somebody got into the house – they must have. Wade wouldn't do it, I didn't do it. Hell, you know it's easy to get into that house. Anybody could walk right in. We've been leaving the windows wide open in the good weather. And we're all heavy sleepers – even the kids. We made it easy.'

Easy for whom? That was the question.

For Norman, who had become accustomed to slipping in and out of the house under cover of darkness – and might have been finding Elf an embarrassment?

For Jeremy, who might have decided there was only one certain way to keep Sylvia from discovering his secret?

There was even Arthur, who might have decided to end his son's indiscretion in the most final way of all.

'You might as well know,' Sinbad said. 'It will come out at the inquest. They've established that she died from suffocation, but they aren't sure how it came about. They're running more tests on the pillow and pillowcase they took away. Seems there ought to be traces of saliva or something if – ' He broke off, swallowing hard.

'It must have been some sort of freak accident,' Crispian said. 'They can't think someone held the pillow over her face until – '

'They aren't saying exactly what they think, but they've got an alternate theory, too.' Sinbad shook his head disbelievingly. 'One they like even better. They think maybe it was one of those damned plastic bags – they're everywhere – you get everything from vegetables to sweaters wrapped up in them. And the warning is like the warning on the cigarette packages, you're so used to it you don't even see it. They think maybe somebody crept in and put the plastic bag over her head while she was still asleep and then later, took it off again and turned her over so it would look like the pillow smothered her.'

'But why should the police think that?' Kay asked.

'Because there's more evidence for that than there is for the pillow – so far.' He grimaced. 'If you can call it evidence. Seems they found one of those little round plastic dots from the air holes caught in her hair. I tried to tell them there was no telling how long it might have been there. It wasn't as if she combed her hair all that often –

'On the other hand – ' he struggled to be fair – 'I suppose it's possible. Those damned air holes are never in the right places.'

'They're to prevent moisture forming inside the bag,' Kay said practically. 'They're not to – ' Her practicality ran out and she could not finish the sentence.

'It couldn't have been suicide, I suppose?' Crispian tried for a solution that would exonerate his friends. 'Some people try it that way. And those bags cling, I understand, once they're over the head. Even if the person has a change of mind, they can't – ' He broke off, the picture in his mind suddenly becoming too vivid.

'Why should Elf want to commit suicide?' Sinbad had had longer to get used to the idea. 'She had everything going for her right now. Best house she's ever been in. Me maybe going to get some money rolling in. The baby? Hell, she was pleased about that. It suited her image – she's the Earth Mother type. She was.

'Besides,' he added glumly. 'If there ever was a bag, it was gone when we found her. She couldn't have killed herself and then taken it off and hidden it.'

'There'll be fingerprints on it when they find it, I should think,' Crispian said thoughtfully. 'That ought to be the right sort of material to hold them.'

'Oh yeah,' Sinbad said. 'You think they're gonna find it, do you? Could be down any sewer by now.' He shrugged. 'Maybe they'll go through every pantry and take away all the plastic bags in the neighbourhood for tests. Go through everybody's garbage bins – messy, nasty job, and still probably they won't find anything.'

Probably they wouldn't. Kay shuddered as another thought struck her. It must have been very easy to slip a plastic bag over the head of a sleeping woman. Another woman could have done it without difficulty. And a woman would have access to a horde of plastic bags and perhaps think of using one more readily than a man. That meant that the women in the neighbourhood weren't to be ruled out. The police would think of that, too.

Had Sylvia found out about Jeremy and Elf? If she imagined the child Elf was carrying were also Jeremy's . . .

And there was Candy, who was almost pathologically jealous of Nick and suspected that the child might be his.

Alice also had her suspicions – correctly, it now appeared. She might have feared that Elf would try to use the baby to force Norman into marriage. She would not have welcomed Elf as a daughter-in-law.

Perhaps that was the most disquieting thought of all. Alice had taken Emma away earlier and Emma was with her now. And Kay wasn't sure where.

'Are you all right?' Kay found Crispian watching her anxiously. Had she gasped or made some sound of distress?

'Yes,' she said. 'I was just . . . thinking.'

'It doesn't bear thinking about,' Sinbad said gloomily, as though they had a choice. 'The inquest is next week. They'll let us know.'

'The recording is next week.' Crispian blurted it out, although he might have been more tactful if he'd taken time to consider.

'Yeah. That, too.' Sinbad seemed to understand. 'The show must go on. But I don't seem to have much heart for it right now.'

'You'll feel better next week,' Crispian urged, perhaps remembering that Sinbad had never been very enthusiastic about the project.

'Sure,' Sinbad said unconvincingly. 'Maybe I will. But

I wouldn't bet on it.' He slumped in his chair. 'There's problems, problems, nothing but problems ahead.'

'But you *will* go ahead with the recording?' Crispian tried to pin him down.

'Oh, sure. If I'm not in jail by then.'

'Jail? Don't be silly. You haven't done anything.'

'Yeah, I know that. Maybe you know it, too – or maybe you just want it to be true. But there's a white woman dead. And a black man and a drug addict living in the same house – and it's not even their house. You think the police are going to waste time going around this nice expensive neighbourhood upsetting all you nice respectable Whiteys when they've got it handed to them on a plate like that?' Sinbad shrugged. 'Maybe they'll decide Wade's a better bet, he wouldn't put up the fight I would. I tell you, man, there's probably only one thing holding them back so far – we're both American citizens and they want to check with the Embassy about complications before they do anything too final. Once they get the go-ahead – '

'But won't the Embassy do anything?'

'Sure. It will give them *carte blanche*.' Sinbad gave a short sharp laugh. 'Especially when they find out Wade was a deserter.'

'But you weren't,' Crispian said softly. It was a question as much as a statement.

'No, not me.' Sinbad sighed. 'I was the dumb one. I played it straight all along. And look where it's got me. No better off than poor old Wade right now. Worse, in fact, because I can see all there is to worry about. Wade's got it lucky there – he just shoots up and he's out of it.'

Crispian remained silent, obviously feeling that Wade would be no loss to the community if the police lighted on him. Certainly, it would be preferable to having any of their friends arrested. But, if Wade hadn't done it, and one of their friends had . . .

Kay felt very thankful that it was for the police to deal with and had nothing to do with her.

Or had it? Crispian was looking increasingly worried. Could it be that he saw more problems than were immediately apparent?

Although there were enough apparent. Like the children. What would happen to them now? Or was Marjorie, with all her Social Services connections, taking care of that? Was that, in fact, why Sinbad had turned to Marjorie rather than to any of the others in the first place?

'I suppose I'd better get back.' Sinbad rose reluctantly.

'Feel free to come over any time,' Crispian urged. 'Just drop in when things begin to get on top of you.'

'Yeah.' Sinbad grinned wryly. 'Long as they'll let me.'

CHAPTER XXII

There followed a curious period of calm. The police appeared, made enquiries, and departed. Life seemed to go on as usual, and yet there was a feeling of impending storm in the atmosphere – as well as the actual storm outside, for the rain had settled in as though determined to make everyone pay for the long fine spell.

Sylvia was convinced that the police were concentrating their efforts elsewhere. Probably backtracking on other squats Elf had been involved in, for it was more reasonable to assume that 'people of that sort' would commit murder than to think that any of the residents of Crozier Crescent could be involved.

Kay was not convinced that the police possessed the complacent snobbishness Sylvia attributed to them, but was just as relieved that they were not continuing their questioning in the immediate vicinity. There were too many uncomfortable secrets to be unearthed – especially Jeremy's. Or did the police know it already? Perhaps that was what they were doing: looking for someone from the past who could provide linking evidence of Jeremy's motive.

The weekend crawled past endlessly, punctuated by *sotto voce* telephone calls from Crispian to various members of the session group he had engaged.

On Monday, Crispian and Sinbad took off first thing in the morning for the recording studio.

By mid-afternoon, the sun had come out, the sky had cleared completely and cautious weather forecasters were once again suggesting that there might be a few more good days in store.

For the first time in days, the squatter children came out

of doors, stepping delicately as cats across the rapidly drying grass. Wade watched them from the kitchen doorway, an apron tied around his waist. He seemed to be taking his new household responsibilities seriously.

The barbecue drew them like a magnet; perhaps it was a symbol to them of the happy time when they had all been together and enjoying a life that had seemed to be opening out before them with a promise of more happy times to come.

'They're going to have another barbecue,' Emma said accusingly at her elbow.

'They can't.' Kay continued watching. 'It's still too wet.'

'It will be dry by dinner-time.' Emma watched Poppy circle the barbecue and test the charcoal with a forefinger. Poppy appeared to be of that opinion too, for she nodded to the others and they went back to the house.

'Why – ?' Emma began.

'Why don't we go to the library?' Kay distracted her. 'You've finished your books, haven't you?'

'Yes,' Emma admitted reluctantly, suspecting that she was being obscurely bribed, but unwilling to refuse the offer.

'Then get your books and come on,' Kay said.

As they passed the Norris house, Emma waved to a small blur behind one of the windows, but the figure drew back without any answering signal. The children had closed ranks and Emma was an outsider. It was not an experience she was accustomed to.

'Can we have tea at Stone's?' Emma asked offhandedly.

'Just what I was thinking.' Kay was grateful that the planned diversion would be a welcome one. 'With some of those lovely cream cakes, and we can buy some more to bring home for dinner.'

'That's good,' Emma said, adding with elaborate unconcern, 'I think having tea at Stone's is *much* nicer than a messy old barbecue, don't you?'

By the time they returned, preparations for the barbecue were well under way. Emma helped unpack the shopping and then withdrew to her room with her pile of books, disdaining to look out of the window at all. She was not going to be rebuffed again.

There was no sign of Crispian or Sinbad. Kay hoped the recording session had started well – and that it would end on schedule. Crispian was a perfectionist about his music and there had been no prior rehearsal time. Even though he swore the session group were good enough not to need more than one or two run-throughs, Sinbad was still largely an unknown quantity. The musicians might be able to do it in one take, but could he? They couldn't afford overtime.

There was no use in worrying, they were committed now and she could only hope for the best. Even if the album were completed in record time, there was no guarantee that it would be taken up by a distributor in the way Crispian hoped, or that it would become a big hit. Or that it would sell at all. Luck also played a big part in these ventures and it would be silly to pretend that it didn't.

This time, she *would* stop thinking about it! She would concentrate on something more cheerful. Or try to.

Kay lingered by the window, smiling as she heard Jasmine laugh aloud at something Wade had mumbled. It was nice to see the children beginning to relax again and trying to get their lives back to normal – or what passed for normal. Of course, Poppy had always done most of the work about the place, so far as Kay could see. Elf had simply been an adult presence, occasionally giving instructions but basically, Kay suspected, creating as much work as she actually helped with.

Not that Wade was any better, although he seemed to

be trying these days. She wondered whether Sinbad was having any success in weaning him off drugs; not that she could blame him if the project had been temporarily shelved in the press of recent events.

Marjorie strolled into the yard and, looking across, waved at Kay. It had been a long time since they had had a chance to have a conversation. Kay decided to interpret the wave as an invitation to go over.

'I *thought* you'd have the courage of your convictions,' Marjorie greeted her.

Kay wasn't sure that she had any convictions at all, far less the ones Marjorie was crediting her with, but she smiled vaguely and looked around.

'I don't expect anyone *else* to join us,' Marjorie said pointedly. 'Although I'm sure there are a few keeping watch from behind their curtains. I *had* thought they might have behaved better over this.'

'Well . . . murder.' Kay found herself apologizing for the others. 'One doesn't expect anything like that in Crozier Crescent.'

'One doesn't *expect* it anywhere, at any time,' Marjorie said severely. 'It will do them good to realize that an exclusive address doesn't guarantee immunity from the shocks that natural flesh is heir to.'

The Crescent had harboured rather more than its share of shocks recently, Kay felt, but forbore to say so. Furthermore, the other residents were *living* through the events, not just standing on one side taking notes.

'They've needed moral support as much as help,' Marjorie said. She sounded defensive, perhaps sensing unspoken criticism.

'They were fortunate to have you,' Kay said truthfully. There was no one else in the neighbourhood so well qualified – or willing – to step into the breach.

'Yes, perhaps.' Marjorie turned away uneasily. 'I

wish there were something more I could do, though.'

'I think you've done splendidly.' Kay followed Marjorie's gaze as she watched the children ferrying the final ingredients from the house. Once again Poppy wrestled with the now-depleted sack of charcoal, Jasmine carried the buns and meat, and Heather brought up the rear with assorted cutlery. This time, however, Wade was carrying a stack of dishes.

'I ought to have bought paper plates for them,' Marjorie said. 'It's just lucky there haven't been more breakages.' She frowned, possibly foreseeing the inevitable moment when the Norrises would arrive to demand an accounting.

'Can't be helped.' Kay dismissed the problem, rightly suspecting that a murder under their roof was going to disturb the Norrises more than any amount of domestic damage.

'I should have thought of it.' Marjorie seemed determined to blame herself for something. 'I'll get some tomorrow.'

Kay watched Poppy toss more charcoal into the barbecue, thrust a few crumpled bits of newspaper amongst it, and light the first match. It spluttered and went out.

Poppy lit another match, this time applying it to one of the bits of paper. It flared briefly, but there was a slight breeze and it was defeated.

Meanwhile, Jasmine had begun splitting buns with a grim determination. Wade slumped to the grass verge and watched the children struggle with an indulgent grin. Heather toddled over and slumped beside him, watching her sisters without enthusiasm.

Poppy kept lighting matches and thrusting them in amongst the coals. The matches kept going out. With dogged persistence, Poppy struck more matches and tried to ignite the charcoal.

A car door slammed at the front of the house. While

Poppy carried on the unequal struggle, the others turned to watch Sinbad, Crispian and Jeremy come into the back-yard.

'We ran into Jeremy,' Crispian said casually. 'And he gave us a lift.' The car keys were dangling from his own hand.

'Mighty neighbourly of him,' Sinbad agreed. His arm was around Jeremy's shoulders, steering him on a straight course. They were obviously trying to sneak him across the yards and into his own house before Sylvia caught them.

'Leasht I could do for nybus . . . nabrus . . . friends,' Jeremy said magnanimously. He missed his footing and sagged against Sinbad heavily.

'Maybe we ought to have us some black coffee before we go any farther.' Sinbad looked down at him worriedly. 'Maybe a hamburger wouldn't be a bad idea, either. What's the matter, honey? Can't you get the fire going?'

'I can get it going.' Poppy came to the end of her matches. In desperation, she set the box alight and dropped it into the barbecue.

'You won't ever get it lit that way.' Sinbad propped Jeremy up in a sun lounge and advanced on the barbecue. 'Let me show you.'

'You stay away!' Poppy said shrilly. 'I can do it myself!'

'Okay, okay.' Sinbad tossed her a box of matches from his pocket. '*Be* independent!'

Poppy caught the matches and nearly spilled them opening the box so fast. She struck one frantically and hurled it into the barbecue.

'Now stop being silly!' Sinbad ordered. 'Let's see what you're doing wrong.' Ignoring her attempts to push him away, he bent over to inspect the barbecue.

'What did you do? Just put some fresh charcoal on top of all that old wet stuff that's been in there for days? That won't work. You ought to know better than that.'

'It will work,' Poppy said. 'It will!'

'Never.' Sinbad lifted the barbecue and carried it over to the edge of the grass. 'We've got to dump all this old stuff out and start fresh with dry charcoal from the sack. Better line the barbecue with some kitchen foil to take care of the dampness, too. Somebody go get me some kitchen foil – '

Jasmine scampered happily away to get it.

'There now – ' Sinbad up-ended the barbecue and dumped its contents beside Wade. 'See, honey, it was all wet through underneath and – '

He broke off. He had been stirring the wet charcoal with his hand. Now he pulled something from it and straightened slowly. He turned, still in slow motion, to look at Poppy. The others could see what he was holding: a wet, soot-streaked plastic bag.

'Oh, Jesus!' Wade dropped his face into his hands. 'Oh-Jesus-oh-Jesus-oh-Jesus,' he whispered.

'Poppy,' Sinbad said incredulously. 'Little Poppy.'

Little Poppy. The expression on her face was confession enough.

Poppy. Kay had thought previously that the method of murder was simple enough and the weapon accessible enough for any woman in the Crescent to have done it; it had not occurred to her that it was so easy a child could have done it.

Poppy. Living in the same house. Who would have thought anything of it if she had been seen entering or leaving her mother's room? And she was able to slip back later to remove the plastic bag. Even the attempt to disguise the crime by turning Elf's face into the pillow spoke of childish clumsiness rather than an adult attempt at concealment.

Poppy, who had stood by the barbecue in the pouring rain, tears streaming down her face because the fire would not ignite into the blaze that would melt away the evidence she had buried under the coals.

Poppy, who had just tried again to destroy the evidence – under their very eyes.

'Oh, Jesus!' Wade lurched to his feet, knocking Heather over. She began to cry quietly. 'We've got to get out of here!'

'Yeah, old buddy,' Sinbad said softly. 'I'm afraid we do.'

'No!' Poppy said. 'No, please – I don't want to go away again. I don't want to. I did it so we could stay. She was going to have another baby and everybody was mad at her – ' Poppy began to sniffle. 'She was always having another baby. And I can't take *care* of any more. I can't! She was just going to go on and on having babies and I'm always the one who has to take care of them – ' Poppy broke down sobbing. 'I couldn't stand it any more!'

Poppy had broken down before, but no one had noticed. They had been sympathetic when she had cried out that she couldn't watch the baby every minute when Heather had thrown the spoon down the waste disposal unit, but they had not recognized the deeper cry of distress. They had remarked that Poppy had done most of Elf's work, but they had not realized the full weight of the burden on those tiny shoulders.

Elf certainly hadn't. Elf had calmly reached out and sequestered anything she had happened to want or need at any given moment, be it a house or a man, without regard to anyone else's needs or desires. She had gone through life unconscious of the problems she inflicted on everyone around her. It had never occurred to her that she was imposing an increasingly impossible strain on a child who ought to have been taken care of rather than doing the caring.

An adult could escape, but Poppy had nowhere else to go. Elf had been a monster of selfishness and she had met a monstrous end. Was it right to blame a child driven beyond her endurance for it?

'Take it easy,' Sinbad said. 'You don't have to go. She's just a kid – ' he appealed to the others. 'They can't do anything to her – ?' He sought Marjorie's eyes.

'Poppy – ' Marjorie avoided his eyes – 'how old are you?'

'I'm ten,' Poppy choked, her sobs diminishing. She raised her head proudly. 'I'll be eleven in December.'

The adults looked at each other in silence. Kay turned to Crispian. He was pale with shock. He put an arm around her, as much for his own comfort as for hers.

'What's the matter?' Sinbad sensed that the answer had been somehow catastrophic. 'What does that mean?'

'It means that she can be held responsible in law for her actions,' Marjorie said. 'Ten is the age of criminal responsibility in this country. If only it had happened last year . . .'

'Last year – ' Poppy looked around at the clean bright houses, the manicured lawns and gardens, the shining curtained windows. 'Last year I didn't know people lived like this.'

Jeremy groaned softly.

'Yeah, now you see it, Whitey!' Sinbad turned on him savagely. 'You see what you've done! But you're a little late, aren't you?'

Too late for Poppy. Too late for Elf.

'Are you planning to come home this evening, Jeremy?' Sylvia's voice shattered the silence. 'Or do you think you'd rather stay out with your . . . friends?'

Stunned, they had not registered Sylvia's approach until she was among them. They looked at her blankly; she might have descended from an alien planet.

'Oh, I say – ' Jeremy struggled forward to the edge of the sun lounge, shocked into sobriety, but not by Sylvia. He scarcely seemed to notice that she was there. 'What are we going to do? We can't – can't – '

'We're not going to,' Sinbad said grimly. 'This is your fault as much as anybody's, Whitey. You didn't care about what happened to your own kid as long as it didn't interfere with *your* nice quiet life. But you owe, Whitey – and now you start to pay!'

'Of course, of course.' Automatically, Jeremy reached for his cheque book.

'Not that way!' Sinbad's whiplash voice halted him. 'That's the easy way. You never made it easy for anybody else!'

'Jeremy!' Sylvia protested. 'Are you going to let that man speak to you like that? What does he mean about Rupert? Of course you've always cared what happened to him.'

Poppy, uncomprehending, still standing alone, began sobbing quietly and despairingly again. Someone ought to go to her and comfort her. Yet none of them made a move.

'It's a whole new ball game, lady,' Sinbad said. 'For everybody. The party's over.'

The kitchen door slammed abruptly. 'Here it is!' Jasmine called out happily, running to Sinbad, waving the foil. She stopped uncertainly, just short of him, seeing the serious expressions on the faces of the adults and her sisters in tears. 'They been naughty girls?' she asked hesitantly.

'Yeah, kinda.' Sinbad dropped to one knee and clutched her to him, burying his face against her throat. 'But you're my good girl. And you're gonna keep on being my good girl – no matter what happens – aren't you, sweetheart?'

'Stay here!' Jasmine clung to him, sensing what was coming. 'Don't go away again. Please.' Tears began to roll down her face.

'Gotta, honey. Believe me, I gotta.' His voice was muffled. 'But I'll be back . . . some time.'

'Sinbad – ' Poppy moved forward awkwardly and rested her hand on his shoulder. 'Sinbad, don't go. Please.'

'I gotta.' He raised his head, then looked away from her quickly. 'Me and Wade – time for us to move on.'

'It's because of me, isn't it?' Poppy was too intelligent to be placated by evasions. 'Stay. I'll tell them what happened. I don't care – '

'No!' Still holding his daughter with one arm, he swept Poppy close to him with the other arm. 'You keep your little mouth shut! You don't tell – we don't tell! If the police ask you any questions, you don't know nothing. You saw nothing, heard nothing, know nothing! Got that? They ask too much, you start to cry and keep on crying – '

'They won't,' Marjorie said. 'They can't press too hard with children. The police can't even question them without a parent or guardian present, perhaps a legal adviser as well. They always find it very unsatisfactory when children are involved in cases.'

'Right!' Sinbad nodded. 'Then Wade and me – we go on the run. Nobody will be surprised. Just what they expected. The police start chasing after us and it will take the heat off here. It don't matter – they'll never catch us. It's a big world out there. Give us a few hours' head start and we'll lose ourselves in it.

'But you – ' He shook Poppy gently. 'You stay here and grow up good, so's it will all be worthwhile. No more funny business, see?'

'We're never going to get that ship now, are we?' Poppy was growing up fast. 'We're never going to sail to all those beautiful islands – ' Sobs choked off her voice.

'Yeah.' Sinbad nodded sadly, there was no use trying to hide it from her. 'Yeah, you blew it, baby.'

Poppy dropped her head on his shoulder. No punishment any Court could inflict would hurt her more than losing Sinbad and the escape he had promised.

Both children clung to him, sobbing bitterly. Heather wound herself around Wade's ankles, adding her howls.

'Gotta go.' Wade lurched forward, impeded by Heather, trying to shake her off. 'Gotta get outa here.'

'Yeah, man.' Sinbad rose to his feet. 'Go pack your stuff. Soon as it gets dark, we're on our way.'

'You're not – ' Sylvia looked around at the others incredulously – 'all going to sit there and let them get away? They've as good as confessed. It's our duty to hold them here and call the police.'

'Sylvia,' Jeremy said through clenched teeth. 'Shut up!'

'Your husband,' Sinbad explained, 'is a little sensitive on the subject of confessions.' Deliberately, he glanced from Poppy's face to Jeremy's face and back again. Sylvia followed his gaze, realization slowly dawning.

'Jeremy!' she whispered, stricken.

'Before you go – ' Crispian deflected attention back to the main problem. 'Don't you think you ought to have a couple of hamburgers?' He nodded meaningly at the crumpled plastic bag Sinbad still held.

'You're right.' Sinbad replaced the barbecue. He took the foil from Jasmine, tore off a piece and lined it, then tumbled in dry charcoal from the sack. By the time he had finished, his hands were empty.

When the coals were glowing, he looked across to Crispian and said, 'Sorry, Cris.'

'Can't be helped,' Crispian said. 'I'll just about be able to manage the cancellation fee for the rest of the session. And, who knows? When I take a good look at what we've actually got, it might be enough for a couple of singles.'

'You do what you want with it,' Sinbad said. 'Any money might ever be coming to me – ' He gestured towards his daughter. 'Buy baby a new pair of shoes.'

'We'll keep an eye on her,' Crispian promised.

'And Poppy – ' Jeremy said belatedly, ten years belatedly. 'I'll look after Poppy.'

'Not in *my* house!' Sylvia snapped back into virulent life. 'Not with Rupert!'

'Er, perhaps not,' Jeremy agreed hastily. Had he, too, caught the sudden flash of hostility in Poppy's eyes as she glanced at Sylvia? It would not be wise – or safe – to offer Poppy shelter under the roof of another female she detested.

'I can take the children,' Marjorie said suddenly. 'That will prevent them from being taken into care and possibly split up.'

'You'd do that?' Sinbad asked. 'They'd let you?'

'The authorities consider that the good of the child is of paramount importance and that it's preferable that children be with someone they know and trust,' Marjorie said. 'They won't mind who takes them, so long as they're looked after well.'

'Okay,' Sinbad said. 'But Wade and me, we'll give you our written authorization to be their guardian. Just to make it more legal, in case there are any difficulties.' He looked at Jeremy with loathing. 'And you'll sign it, too, Whitey. Just so's I can be sure there won't be a fast shuffle somewhere after I've gone.'

'I'll sign,' Jeremy said. 'I'll help financially, as well.' He looked as though he had seen daylight at the end of a long tunnel. One tunnel, anyway.

'Jeremy!' Sylvia said. 'I demand an explanation!'

'Go back to the house, Sylvia,' Jeremy said firmly. 'I'll be along later. We can discuss as much as you need to know then.'

Sylvia opened her mouth to protest, but closed it again as she encountered Jeremy's eyes. Momentarily, they were the eyes of a stranger – an older, wiser, sadder stranger. She looked helplessly to the others for support and found none.

'I'm going home,' Sylvia announced abruptly, as though it had been her own idea. 'I'll expect you . . . when you can tear yourself away!' She turned and left.

'Jeremy will help,' Marjorie assured Sinbad in a tone that indicated that Jeremy would be of more help than he had perhaps visualized.

'He'd better,' Sinbad said flatly. 'But you – ' He looked at her uncertainly. 'This is awfully good of you. But are you sure – ?'

'The children have been moved about too much as it is,' Marjorie cut in firmly. 'They need a period of calm and stability. I have a bigger house than I need. It won't be too many years before they're of age and can take over their own lives. They'll be getting married before we know it.'

'*I* won't.' Poppy edged closer to Marjorie. 'I don't ever want to do anything but live alone in a nice house like other people.' The tears were drying on her face, pale and stark as a death mask, a child so emotionally battered that she could visualize only a cold sterility as her ideal state. 'With nobody else to clutter it up ever, or make me go somewhere else when I don't want to.'

Kay remembered suddenly the old epitaph on children's tombstones: '*If I were to be so soon done for, I don't know what I was begun for.*' There were more ways than one of 'doing for' a child, she thought bleakly.

Was Poppy done for? Or could Marjorie apply enough of that sociology and psychology to reclaim her for society? Letting the Social Services take her into care and ship her off to a foster home or a series of foster homes would only exacerbate that dangerous alienation from the human race already so deeply ingrained in Poppy. It would be a severe test of Marjorie's theories, but it was a better chance for Poppy than any of the alternatives.

'There you are, man.' Sinbad looked up as Wade

returned, having left his rucksack in readiness by the back door. 'That's good. Now suppose you cook us some hamburgers while I pack. Everybody just keep looking nice and natural, no sudden moves, nothing suspicious. When it's good and dark, we'll light out – and they can draw their own conclusions at the inquest.'

'The inquest will probably be adjourned,' Crispian said. '"Pending further enquiries".'

'Which is the English way of saying the case is closed – or as good as.' Sinbad turned away. Jasmine tagged behind him as he went back to the house and he did not attempt to dissuade her.

'We – we'll discuss arrangements in a few days,' Jeremy told Marjorie. 'When the fuss will have died down.'

'Yes,' Marjorie said. 'We will.'

'I'd better – ' Jeremy began backing towards his own house. 'I'd better go and see what Sylvia's doing. We don't want her telephoning anyone right now.'

'And we must go and give Emma her dinner.' Kay felt that she was abandoning a sinking ship, but if they were to keep everything looking normal, they couldn't huddle together conspiratorially any longer. 'If we can do anything, please let us know.'

'All right,' Marjorie said. 'I'll stay here with the children tonight, I think, and move them into my house tomorrow. I can tell the police that I fell asleep babysitting and hadn't realized that the men never came back from the pub.'

Emma took herself off to watch television, grumbling at the curious unresponsiveness of her parents to all her attempts at conversation that evening.

Kay and Crispian sat in the darkened kitchen with the windows open, listening to the glorious voice rippling out in farewell:

'We must walk this lonesome valley,
'We gotta walk it by ourselves,
'Nobody else can walk it for us,
'We gotta walk it by ourselves . . .'

The notes of the Spiritual died away on the quiet night air. Marjorie and the children sat silently around the glowing coals of the barbecue. The silence lengthened, cold and lonely and unbroken.

'They're gone,' Kay sighed softly.

'Yes,' Crispian said. 'The police *will* be pleased.'

M
BAB Babson, Marian
C.1 So soon done f

$15.95

	DATE		
✓	8-14-13		

MAR 3 1993
JUL 1 2 1993
AUG 2 3 1993
SEP 7 1993
APR 1 1994
DEC 16 1994
FEB 2 1995
AUG 1 5 1995
MAR 1 5 1996
APR 0 6 1996
SEP 1 0 1997

Mar. 9

© THE BAKER & TAYLOR CO.